And then suddenly on the floor above me a light shone from an open door, and I saw Aunt Dorothy standing there in her long white velvet dressing-gown edged with sable.

And there was a man with her, but for a moment I could not see him, and then I heard her say in almost a whisper:

"Darling . . . you need not go yet! It is quite early."

"I must. Do be careful—someone will hear you," he answered.

With that he turned and walked quickly down the stairs.

And I stood absolutely still, too stunned even to think . . . for as he passed me I saw it was Harry.

AN INNOCENT
IN MAYFAIR

Barbara Cartland

PYRAMID BOOKS ▲ NEW YORK

AN INNOCENT IN MAYFAIR

A PYRAMID BOOK

Copyright © 1976 by Barbara Cartland

Pyramid edition published January 1976

ISBN: 0-515-03985-3

Library of Congress Catalog Card Number: 75-35472

Printed in the United States of America

Pyramid Books are published by Pyramid Communications, Inc. Its trademarks, consisting of the word "Pyramid" and the portrayal of a pyramid, are registered in the United States Patent Office.

PYRAMID COMMUNICATIONS, INC.
919 Third Avenue, New York, N.Y. 10022

AUTHOR'S NOTE

I wrote this novel because it was what I discovered Mayfair to be like when I came out in the early twenties.

The Night-Clubs and most of the characters in the story were real people and the atmosphere is correct, only I had fair hair and no money!!

REFLECTION ONE

1923

I'm terribly excited about everything, but rather frightened.

I've looked forward to this so long that now it is actually happening to me I can hardly believe it is true.

It's years and years since I saw Aunt Dorothy—in fact, long before I went to school. I do wish it was Mummy who was going to bring me out.

I feel half the fairy stories ought to be written about wicked stepfathers. Not that mine is really wicked—in fact he is rather a pet—but it is terribly unfeeling of him to be Governor in such an outlandish spot, and for so many years.

I hated leaving the nuns. They were really very kind, although, of course, with all the rest, I have grumbled for two years about them.

Why does one always grumble against authority, good or bad? I wonder.

I never thought it would be so upsetting, leaving them. Little Sister Agnes once told me that she dreaded the beginning of term because it brought all sorts of new girls who might be unsettling and difficult.

I wonder if I have been unsettling and difficult? It is so hard to judge one's self.

Anyway, here I am, with an exciting, rather sick feeling inside me.

The sick feeling I have just had on the boat was quite bad enough, but this is even more upsetting, I think—it makes me feel as if my inside was in a lift, and my toes were wriggling.

Another five minutes before we get to London; then it is all going to begin.

REFLECTION TWO

I can't make up my mind if I like Aunt Dorothy or not. She seems so fantastic, and quite unlike anything I imagined.

I suppose she must be terribly attractive to men—there certainly seem to be plenty in the house the whole time.

The house is too lovely. I must say it has impressed me awfully. I love the Chinese Drawing-room, with the red lacquer furniture against the white walls and the heavenly embroidered curtains.

It seems exactly the right setting for Aunt Dorothy, with her dark hair, tiny oval face and black eyes.

I wonder who all the men were who were there when I arrived?

I've never been so frightened in my life as when I went up the staircase and the butler absolutely shouted across what seemed to me the longest room I have ever seen:

"Miss Maxine, My Lady!"

There were masses of people grouped about, all laughing and screaming remarks at the tops of their voices. Do they ever talk quietly, I wonder?

Then I saw Aunt Dorothy.

She is so small and compact that she makes me feel large and *gauche,* and, of course, I knew, anyway, that my clothes were all wrong, but somehow, compared with hers, they seemed absolutely terrible:

She said:

"Maxine, dear! I am so pleased to see you, and I do hope you will enjoy being here."

Everybody screamed at once, before I could say anything, about how absurd it was for her to bring out a niece when she looked so young, and I felt so stupid that I just murmured something in the way of 'Thank you', and asked if I could go to my room.

My bedroom is simply charming, like the rest of the house, and I look straight into the gardens of the Square.

My great friend, Thelma, knows everything, and she told me that Grosvenor Square was one of the smartest and richest places to live in in London.

I expect it is, for I know that Grandpa was awfully rich when he died, and he left all his money divided between Daddy and Aunt Dorothy.

As Daddy is dead, I suppose I shall get some of his money when I am twenty-one—at least, I have always heard so. In the meantime, I do hope they will let me have a little with which to buy some clothes.

I wonder if I am good-looking?

It would be too frightful if I go to dances and nobody dances with me, except duty dances, like we had to at the Convent with the fat German girls, who were so boring and heavy on hand.

Thelma's brother, Tommy, said I had an 'unsettling' face. I do not know what he meant by that. No, that is not true. At least I think I do know—I must not pretend, even to myself. I loathe people who pretend to themselves.

He is very odd about it; but, of course, being an artist, he has different ideas from most people.

He had the most lovely studio in Paris, and Thelma used to be allowed to take me there on half-holidays. I can see it now:

A jumble of antique furniture he had picked up on the quays—Louis Quinze and Louis Quatorze—and some perfectly lovely Buhl, mixed up with easels and artists' properties.

He had lots of Spanish shawls and rolls of silk, which

Thelma and I used to drape ourselves in and beg him to paint us, but he never would.

He only used to make rude remarks about our idea of a picture.

Personally—only I did not dare say so—I did not think much of his idea of one!

Last year he was hung on the line in the *Salon des Indépendants,* and it was called 'Recumbent Figure on a Hot Day', and was a picture of a pea-green woman under an umbrella apparently suffering from an attack of net-tlerash.

I thought it awful and perfectly hideous, but the critics praised it like anything, because Thelma showed me some of the cuttings in the art papers.

One day I asked Tommy what type my face belonged to.

We were talking about features, and he had said that Thelma was distinctly an American-Indian type, and he answered, quite crossly:

"Oh, your face is just unsettling, Maxine!"

"Tell me what you mean?" I asked.

He said no, and I begged:

"Please Tommy," coaxingly, like when I asked the Mother Superior for an extra treat, and he turned round quite crossly and said:

"Damn it all, Maxine, you are as annoying as a mosquito!"

Then he took my chin and tilted my head back, and quite suddenly I had the strangest feeling, as if something thrilling was going to happen.

Tommy looked so strange, and rather cross, but I was not a bit frightened, only just that strange feeling.

Then suddenly he took his hand away and rushed to the other end of the room and started playing the piano.

Just for a moment I could think of nothing to say, and then the noise of the gramophone and the piano was too terrific, and we all started laughing, and he never said any more.

It seems ages since I last saw him, though actually it is only about eight hours. He and Thelma saw me off at the *Gare du Nord* and gave me some lovely roses to wear. They are crushed now, and rather faded.

I must have seemed awfully stupid, because I was crying so frightfully. I hated leaving Thelma, who had been like a sister to me.

She is going to America, to make her *début* in the 'fall'—whenever that may be.

Just as the train was going, I held out my hand to Tommy, and he kissed it, just like a Frenchman, and said:

"Au revoir, Maxine. I shall come and see you very soon—as soon as you are grown up!"

I do not know what he meant by that, because I really am quite grown up now. After all, I am nearly nineteen, and that seems terribly old when you think that most girls come out at seventeen nowadays.

In fact I have missed nearly two years, but Mummy was frightfully firm about it, and I cannot help thinking it was because she could not bring me out herself.

I have a strange idea—I cannot think why, but it is persistent—that Mummy does not quite approve of Aunt Dorothy.

She has never said so, but they were not tremendous friends when Mummy and I were living together in Somerset. But then, all our friends lived around us there.

We were terribly happy—at least I was, because I had a pony, and Mummy had a garden and hens and chickens, and if she wanted to hunt there were always people willing to mount her.

And then one day she came back from a Luncheon party all flushed and excited, with a tall, quite good-looking man in an oldish sort of way, and she said:

"Ralph, dear, this is my little Maxine."

I was not so very little, but I find people always talk about their only children as if they were pathetic.

Then Mummy said:

"Maxine, dear, this is my old friend, Sir Ralph Strange, who has just returned from abroad."

I said, "How do you do?"

And he said, "How do you do?" looking at Mummy all the time, and Mummy said, "Will you go and feed the chickens for me, darling?"

It was only four o'clock, and the chickens were never fed until six. But I guessed it was an excuse, so I went away and left them alone.

12

I found Martha in the kitchen, and she said:

"The gipsy said there'd come a wedding to the house— you mark my words, Miss Maxine!"

"What gipsy?" I asked. "And whose wedding?"

"The gipsy who was here last week," Martha answered, "from the Fair."

Then I remembered seeing her, but I asked again:

"Whose wedding, Martha?"

"Whose but your Ma's," she answered.

I would not believe her—but the gipsy was right, for a month later they were married, I was sent to Paris, and they left for the outlandish spot where he is Governor.

It was all so quickly over and done with that until I was actually in the Convent I did not realise I would not see Mummy again for years, and that I was alone amongst strangers.

Even now there is nearly another two years to go before she comes home, so Aunt Dorothy had promised to bring me 'out'.

Aunt Dorothy is always in the *Tatler* and all the other papers. They always head her photographs:—

'A Beautiful London Hostess', or 'The Beautiful Wife of a Well-known Politician'.

I suppose she is very beautiful, and she certainly has marvellous taste, to judge by the house and her appearance.

I wish I knew a little more about the people I am going to meet.

I wonder if I shall make lots of friends? I wish Thelma was with me. She is so brave, and is not frightened of anyone.

But I'm quite frankly shaking with fright in case I do something wrong, but I don't expect I shall.

Anyway, it is no use worrying!

REFLECTION THREE

Everyone seems incredibly difficult to understand and I am not certain if I am enjoying myself or if I am frightfully unhappy.

Last night was a whirl of impressions, and I do not seem to have got any of them very straight. I know one thing, and that is that I do not like Aunt Dorothy very much.

I think she means to be kind, but at the same time she seems rather hard, brilliant and uncomfortable to live with, like trying to use a diamond as a pillow.

She had ordered me a lovely dress for last night, really very pretty—white, of course, as I am a *débutante*, but embroidered here and there with green leaves, and a lovely frothy tulle skirt.

I felt frightfully sophisticated in it, and it really did look nice with my red hair.

Mabel—Aunt Dorothy's maid—did my hair very low at the back of my neck. She was very pleased with the result, and so was I.

Anyway, when I came downstairs there were heaps of people there to dinner, all marvellously dressed, but talking what seemed to me a language of their own.

Every other word was 'darling' or 'divine', and they had extraordinary expressions which did not seem very funny, but whenever anyone uttered them the rest screamed with laughter.

I refused a cocktail when it was offered me, but Aunt Dorothy said:

"Nonsense, you had better start as you mean to go on."

It was the first time I had had one, and I can't say I liked it much. I drank half, and hid the rest behind a photograph frame when no one was looking!

Mabel had told me that dinner was to be at half past eight, but it was nearly half past nine before everyone had arrived.

I should have thought it was dreadfully rude for a man to be late, but no one seemed to care when someone they all called 'Harry' arrived long after nine o'clock and just said:

"Please forgive me. I was enjoying my bath so much!"

Aunt Dorothy said:

"Darling, I'm furious," but you could tell by her eyes she was not a bit really.

Harry seems the nicest of all the men here, and apparently he is the most important, for they all made a terrible fuss of him, and laughed at all his jokes and listened to everything he said.

He is tall, and awfully good-looking, but he has a funny manner—rather aloof—and if I did not know he was such a friend I should say he was almost rude to them—sort of insolent, as if he secretly despised the whole lot of them.

Perhaps I am quite wrong, because he said lots of charming things to all the women, especially to Aunt Dorothy, and I may be imagining the idea that he did not really mean them.

The women were all most wonderfully dressed, and had the most wonderful jewels.

There was one girl who I thought was years older than me, but I found she was only a last year's *débutante*.

She seemed so much older that I thought she was nearly Aunt Dorothy's age. She was very painted, and wore huge drop diamond earrings and masses of bracelets.

Afterwards I said to Aunt Dorothy that I thought she was much older than she was, and Aunt Dorothy laughed and said:

"Oh, she will get younger in a year or two. They always start by trying to be Mrs. Methuselah."

I think I know what she means, because I keep wishing I was much older myself and knew how everything happened.

It would all be such a wonderful adventure if one was not frightened of being *gauche* and making a fool of oneself!

It is so difficult to know what to say. No one seems to finish a sentence, and they all talk at once, and never talk about any particular subject, but just about people or things, and tell incredible stories about things happening to themselves.

After dinner we all went on to the Embassy Club, which is quite the smartest and most *chic* place to dance in London.

It was absolutely crowded, and at first I was just a little bit disappointed, having heard so much about it.

It was just a long yellow room, with not very pretty lighting, but when I had sat down, looked about and listened to what my party were saying I realised that everyone present was terrifically important or notorious.

Aunt Dorothy told me who one or two of the people were and then I danced with a man in the party called Cecil, who apparently knew everybody.

They all said, "Darling, when are you going to photograph me?" as we went round, and he told me who the people were and was frightfully funny about them.

There were at least three women in the room who each thought she was the best-dressed woman in Europe, and the joke was that two of them were wearing similar dresses, which made it difficult to decide.

There were two or three married couples who had separated and come together again, and there was frightful excitement because a young man had not brought the woman that he brought every Thursday night.

It all sounded rather complicated, and I could not help thinking that I would rather the floor was emptier and I could have danced more.

I danced with Harry, and he was awfully sweet to me, and said, "Are you feeling frightened?" quite seriously, not a bit in the half-teasing, rather sarcastic manner in which the rest of the party spoke to me, as if I were a pet dog or somebody else's baby.

16

I wonder why *débutantes* have that effect on other people?

"Yes, I am, rather," I answered.

"Never mind," he said, "you will settle down in a day or two, and find things much more amusing."

I said "Thank you" to him, and he said:

"Do not thank me. I feel awfully sorry for you, planted in the middle of this crowd!"

I did not like to ask him what he meant, but I felt somehow it was not very complimentary to Aunt Dorothy.

We danced round and round, except when we were stopping to talk to all the people who seemed to want to talk to him, and lots of them stared at me in the most surprised manner.

One woman said:

"Goodness me, Harry, what's this?"

"May I introduce Dorothy's niece?" he replied.

"Oh!" she remarked, in a relieved yet disappointed tone, as if she had thought something quite different.

We danced for a long time, and he was awfully nice, and told me about London and lots of things I should enjoy.

I said to him:

"What do you do?"

"Nothing at the moment," he replied, "because my father has not been dead very long, and I am getting the estate settled."

The band went on playing for ages, and we danced until it stopped, but when we went back to the table Aunt Dorothy did not seem at all pleased to see us. She said, in quite an acid tone:

"I should like to dance with you now, Harry, or have you taken a liking to children's parties?"

He did not answer her or say anything, but got up and walked over to the next table, where there were some friends of his, and talked to them for ages and ages.

Aunt Dorothy stared at his back and kept tapping her fingers on the table as if she was frightfully irritated about something.

At about half past twelve, when I was absolutely dropping with tiredness, after the long day and having been so

17

sick on the boat, we all got up, and I thought we were going home.

But not a bit of it!

We went on to a funny little Night-club, where we all signed our names as we went in. Only not our real names; just 'Miss Brown' or 'Jones', or 'Smith'.

It seemed very stupid, because the man at the door knew exactly who Aunt Dorothy was, and called her 'My Lady', even though she had written down 'Mrs. Smith' in the book!

We went down a long flight of steps and found ourselves in a small room with a very low ceiling.

The band consisted of two pianos and a drum, which made a terrific noise.

Everybody was dancing quite madly. The place was full of people, lots of whom we had already seen at the Embassy, and they all waved and screamed to us.

When we were seated, a waiter came up and said:

"What will you drink?"

Someone ordered champagne and it came in a large glass jug. That was because they were frightened of being raided.

It did not seem very amusing to me, but perhaps I was rather tired.

One or two people were especially noisy, and threw the waiters' trays about.

All the women danced most awfully energetically, their hair flying; it looked very funny when they had been rather sedate and languid at the Embassy.

While we were there, quite an oldish man came up to Aunt Dorothy and asked to be introduced to me.

They all laughed, and said:

"Hugo, you are incorrigible!"

"This is Maxine—and this is Lord . . ."

I did not catch his name, because everybody screamed at once, and the woman opposite said:

"Don't you have anything to do with him, Maxine! He is dreadfully naughty . . . aren't you, Hugo?"

One of the other men said:

"You ought to know, Ada!"

And she made a face at him, and did not mind a bit.

18

Lord Hugo—whatever his other name was—said to me:
"Will you come and dance?"

I could not very well refuse, so I got up, feeling rather embarrassed, as they all laughed and called out remarks.

He must have been very good-looking when he was young, but he had rather a bleary look now.

I did not like him frightfully, he held me much too tight so that I could hardly breathe—and said:

"I think you are adorable."

There did not seem anything to say to that except "Thank you," and he went on:

"Will you let me see something of you, and be a little kind to me?"

I said, very politely, I did not think I could make any plans until I knew what Aunt Dorothy had arranged for me.

"Oh, that will be all right," he said. "I will talk to Dolly myself. You let me show you all the exciting places in London. And, if I do, will you be kind to me?" he repeated.

I said I supposed I was always kind to everybody—why should I not be kind to him?

He laughed a little at that, then squeezed me even tighter, and said:

"You are sweet!"

I thought he was very unpleasant, and I hated being squeezed, so I said I was tired and wanted to go back to the table.

"When shall I see you again?" he said, and I said I was afraid I could not make any plans.

"I shall ring you up tomorrow," he said, and squeezed my hand, adding:

"I cannot let you go—we must dance again."

I said, "No, really, I am tired," and went back to the table.

He still followed me, trying to insist on yet another dance, so I said quite firmly to Aunt Dorothy that I was frightfully tired, and might I go home.

"Good gracious," she said, "these young things cannot even stay the course so easily as the old ones!"

Then Lord Hugo said:

"I will take her home for you, if you do not want to go, Dolly."

I thought this was awful, so I said it did not matter. I would wait until Aunt Dorothy went home.

"Nonsense," she said. "If you are tired, you had better go. Hugo can easily drop you—it is on his way."

I felt the one thing in the world I did not want to do was to go home with this horrible old man.

I started to say I really did not want to, when Harry said:

"I am tired now, so I will come too."

"Oh, wait five minutes more, Harry," said Aunt Dorothy, "and you can take me."

"No," he said, "I think I will go with Maxine and Hugo."

Everyone seemed to call each other by their Christian names in this party.

Aunt Dorothy said:

"Really, Harry, I asked you to wait for me."

"So sorry, dear, but I am absolutely dead," he answered.

I knew she was perfectly furious, because she did not speak to me any more, but went off to dance with another man in the party, and Lord Hugo did not seem very pleased either.

We got into a taxi in complete silence, and drove to Grosvenor Square, hardly speaking at all.

Lord Hugo said:

"I shall ring you up in the morning," and then "Good night," and tried to squeeze my hand again.

But I took it away very quickly, and Harry got out and opened the door for me.

On the doorstep he said:

"Good night—and sleep well, *débutante!*"

I said, "Good night—and thank you terribly," and I think he knew that I was really thanking him for having come back with us, for he smiled and said:

"That's all right!"

I wanted to add that I hoped Aunt Dorothy would not be very angry with him, but I thought perhaps I had better not.

He raised his hat and jumped back into the taxi before I could say any more.

20

REFLECTION FOUR

I have had a talk with Aunt Dorothy!

She sent for me about ten o'clock, when she was called.

I had been awake for ages, and I wanted to get up, but Mabel said no, I had better rest, and, anyway, there was no fire or anything ready downstairs.

So I read the newspapers she brought me with my breakfast. It does seem funny to have breakfast in bed after the scramble at the Convent! How I hated that bell at seven-thirty—I was always late!

I was just getting up to have my bath when Aunt Dorothy sent for me.

Her bedroom is jade green, with orange silk curtains, and the largest gold bed I have ever seen.

Her sheets were apricot-coloured, and she wore the most lovely dressing-jacket, covered in ostrich feathers, of the same colour.

She did not look half as young as I thought.

She has rather a yellow skin without rouge, and her eyes seem quite tiny without make-up round them.

She was giving orders to her secretary when I arrived, and being so cross, but she smiled at me and said:

"Good morning, Maxine," and then:

"That will be all, Miss Roberts, and for goodness sake use your brains this time, if you have any."

21

Miss Roberts, a poor weak-looking girl with greasy hair, and glasses, absolutely cringed and fled from the room.

"Now, Maxine," Aunt Dorothy said briskly, "I want to talk to you about yourself. Sit down somewhere."

I got a chair and brought it near the bed.

Aunt Dorothy settled a lot of lace pillows comfortably behind her.

Then she said:

"You are a pretty child. I suppose you know that?"

I blushed, because it was not what I expected her to say.

"Never be ashamed of your assets," she continued sharply as I did not reply. "If you do not put a good value on yourself, no one else is likely to, and that is what I want to talk to you about.

"I am to bring you out, which means introduce you to nice people and eventually find you a husband.

"Do not argue!" she added, as I tried to protest. "Of course you have to marry, and the sooner the better these days, with so few decent men about, and such competition among the women. I only hope you have got sex-appeal; however that remains to be seen.

"What I want to make clear to you is that you must look after yourself. Very few girls are closely chaperoned these days, and even if they were, I really cannot spend my life at private dances or sitting on the dais at country balls.

"You must fit yourself in with my friends and my interests. Your mother, of course, is all for you moving in what years ago we used to call the 'best circles'—they do not exist today.

"There are a few bores, I believe, who still give kid-gloved dances, and where flocks of *débutantes* giggle girlishly over lemonade, but you certainly will not meet any eligible young men there.

"A few half-baked youths, perhaps, but no man, unless he was crazy, would go to such a party.

"With me and my friends you will certainly meet what the gossip columns call 'Society', but you must expect to look after yourself. I cannot rush round defending your virtue and your little innocent mind.

"You will soon learn to be independent, and the sooner

the better. You are not a baby, Maxine, you are nearly nineteen; and, personally, I think it absurd that you have been left at school so long.

"But you can speak up for yourself, and with some decent clothes there is no reason why you should not be a success.

"After all, you will be quite an heiress, and that is a help these days, but if you were as rich as Croesus I could not make you a success unless you have it in you.

"Society nowadays consists of the people who are amusing; it does not matter who they are or where they have come from, but if they go well at a party they are asked everywhere—and if they are bores they stay at home.

"Remember that, Maxine, and I hope you will have a lovely time. I am only too glad, remember, to give my advice any time you want it, and you will have an allowance every month for your clothes—see Miss Roberts about it. Now, darling, you understand, don't you?"

"Yes, Aunt Dorothy, and thank you for having me."

"That is all right," she answered. "Now run away, dear. I have got a lot of telephoning to do."

As she spoke, the telephone bell rang, and I left the room as she was saying:

"Oh, it's you, darling . . ."

It is so strange, all she said to me, so unlike what I expected.

I do hope I've got sex-appeal. I wonder how one knows. I do wish one could take the temperature of one's sex-appeal with a thermometer.

I quite see Aunt Dorothy does not want me on her hands very long. I only wish Mummy was here—she would explain such a lot of things I want to know.

But somehow, in spite of what Aunt Dorothy said, I feel I shall never be brave enough to ask her.

REFLECTION FIVE

Uncle Lionel is a darling. He is tall and awfully distinguished-looking; a little bit grey at the sides of his hair; and has that worried, rather anxious look which seems to belong to the diplomatic and political professions.

He generally seems a little absentminded, as if half his thoughts were somewhere else, but he is terribly nice to me, and said I was nearly as pretty as Mummy was at my age—not quite, because he had always adored her. But he thought I should 'do very nicely'.

He asked what we had done so far since my arrival, and I told him that Aunt Dorothy had bought me heaps of clothes and I had been to several Night-clubs.

He said:

"Do not think that is the beginning and end of London, little Maxine, because it is not. Come along to the House one day, and I will show you a more serious side."

I said I would adore to, and he has promised to take me to lunch at the House of Commons next Wednesday, and to show me all over it, and the Lords as well.

I do think he is terribly sweet, but I do not think Aunt Dorothy thinks so. She is awfully petulant with him, and she said:

"Oh, Lionel always upsets the atmosphere as soon as he arrives."

In the afternoon we do very little.

Occasionally I have a fitting, or we drive to the hairdresser's, but generally Aunt Dorothy plays bridge or backgammon until cocktail-time, and then after that everything is a whirl of gaiety till the early hours of the morning.

I see a lot of Harry.

I have found out now that his name is Sir Harold Standish, that he has just come into the baronetcy, and that he is awfully rich, and what Aunt Dorothy's crowd call a 'catch'.

Mona, the very sophisticated *débutante* whom I met the first night I arrived, tells me that all the girls adore him, but he only has *affaires* with married women.

I cannot help thinking that Aunt Dorothy likes him very much indeed.

She always talks to him in a funny kind of intimate voice, and gets awfully cross and irritable if he talks too long to anyone else when she is there.

Harry does not seem to treat her specially differently from anyone else, for he always keeps that same aloof manner that I noticed the first night.

I have been 'out' nearly a fortnight now, and Aunt Dorothy already seems rather bored with having to take me everywhere.

On two or three occasions she has sent me to dances with quite strange people, and I must say they have been awfully kind, introducing me to people and looking after me.

In fact I am not certain that I do not enjoy the dances without Aunt Dorothy the best.

But a most extraordinary thing happened the other night.

I had been to a dance given by a Lady Brooks, with Mona, chaperoned by Mona's mother, and as the party was getting towards the end a rather nice young man called David—I never heard his other name—came up and said to me and another girl in the party:

"Do you two want to come to a really amusing show?"

Of course we said yes, and he said:

"Well, John and I are going on to a party in Chelsea. If you like to come we will take you along."

Of course we said we would love it, and we told Mona's

mother we were going home, and that David and his friend would drop me.

She said, "All right," absentmindedly, and we left— feeling a little bit guilty, but quite determined to see all the fun!

The party was given in a huge studio somewhere off the King's Road. It was beautifully decorated, and must have cost a lot of money.

When we arrived, a band was blaring in the corner, and nearly everybody there was dressed in Victorian costume. Round the room were lots of little tables covered with crocheted table-centres and aspidistras.

Someone tore up to us and said, "How do you do?"— dressed in a bright pink gingham frock with a poke bonnet, and imagine my surprise when I found it was a man!

His get-up was so perfectly done that if one had not heard his voice one would have thought it really was a woman.

Inside, the studio was a racket of noise and laughter.

There was a huge bar at the end, and everyone was drinking champagne, or what at first I took to be water, and afterwards discovered to be gin.

There were about twenty couples dancing, all in fancy dress; some beautiful ones, but mostly rather fantastic, or so they seemed, until I realised that what looked like peculiar women were really men in disguise.

One guest had come as a Can-Can girl of the eighteen-nineties, with a red wig and a huge bow on the top, and his short sequined dress looked so funny against his very brawny bare shoulders and muscular arms.

No one took the slightest notice of me or of Mary, the other girl.

A lot of the men had assumed high, soprano voices for the occasion, and they rushed at each other saying:

"Darling, darling, do dance with me!"

I thought they acted awfully well, except that nearly all the men who were dressed as women danced with each other, which seemed out of keeping with the character.

However, they all seemed to be enjoying themselves frightfully, but no one asked us to dance, and we felt a little out of it.

26

So we went and sat upstairs in a kind of gallery which overlooked the studio, and David and John brought us some champagne, and we leant over the railing and watched the fun below.

There was one awfully good-looking man dressed as a sailor, and he started to dance with a strange-looking woman who apparently had not bothered to come in fancy dress.

She seemed rather overexcited, for she kept on trying to kiss him, and then two other men, one of whom was dressed as a Victorian schoolgirl, rushed up to him and said:

"But you promised to dance with us!"

And then, I do not know why, they all got awfully angry and shouted rude things at one another, and even went so far as to slap one another's faces.

But it must have been only a joke, because the man who was dressed as the schoolgirl pretended to burst into tears and rushed away into a corner, and we all laughed, and I said to David:

"How clever of him to keep up the character of his dress!"

But David looked at John and said:

"I think it is time we went home."

And Mary said sort of meaningly:

"Yes, I think it is."

"Oh no! I am enjoying so much," I said, but they insisted and we went away.

As we got outside the studio, in the little entrance hall was a young man fast asleep on the floor. I said:

"What a queer place to sleep in!"

But David said, "Leave him alone," and hurried me into the taxi.

It was a frightfully strange party, and somehow I felt we ought not to have been there; perhaps the people were not frightfully good class.

Anyway, David said I was not to tell Aunt Dorothy he had taken us, so of course I said I would not, although I do not suppose Aunt Dorothy would have cared one way or another.

I did tell Uncle Lionel something about it, and he became very serious, and said I was never to go to parties again without telling Aunt Dorothy.

I was sorry I had been such a fool to mention it.

But, thinking it over, I do feel it was a rather strange collection of people, and perhaps even Aunt Dorothy's friends would not have cared for them.

I met a rather interesting man at dinner last night who was so amusing.

He is called Lord Weatherley, and apparently he is a great sportsman and a frightfully good cricketer.

They all called him 'Timmy' and laughed at everything he said; and when he paid me a compliment Aunt Dorothy said:

"Now, Timmy, behave! Maxine is only a *débutante,* and you know you've been barred the schoolroom for years."

"Don't you know I'm a reformed character?" Timmy asked, and everybody screamed and said they hadn't noticed it.

"Perhaps Maxine will reform me," he went on. "Will you, Maxine?"

I hate being asked questions of that sort, because I always feel I ought to make a frightfully witty answer, and yet I can't think of anything to say.

So I merely said I thought Aunt Dorothy could reform him far better than I could, and Timmy roared with laughter, and said:

"Oh, she tried, and failed, years ago, didn't you, Dolly?"

She did not answer, but went away to get him a cocktail. Anyway, it took everybody's attention off me for a moment or so.

I still can't get used to the noise they make and the way remarks spring up from nowhere and no one seems to answer them.

It is rather like living in an old-fashioned kaleidoscope—the colours and patterns keep changing, and before you have time to realise one it is altered.

Uncle Lionel asked me what I thought of Aunt Dorothy's friends, and I said the only one I really liked was Harry. He murmured something under his breath which I did not hear, but he did not look very pleased, so I think perhaps he dislikes him.

28

Aunt Dorothy's greatest woman friend is someone they all call 'Baba'.

She is very small and thin, with huge eyes and golden hair, which is a mass of curls at the back and quite straight over her forehead.

She has a most amusing way of talking, and calls everybody 'old boy' or 'old girl'. She has a quite oldish man, who is devoted to her, and never talks to anyone else if he can listen to her.

I thought at first he was her husband, but apparently her husband lives in Paris, and the oldish man, who is called Derek, is only a great friend.

I asked Aunt Dorothy if Baba ever saw her husband, and she said, "Not often", and I asked why not, because Baba is so pretty.

"Oh, he doesn't care for women much," she answered.

I did not quite see what that had to do with Baba, but as Aunt Dorothy changed the subject I had to leave it at that.

We were all drinking cocktails the other afternoon when suddenly Lord Hugo arrived.

I had not seen him since the first night.

"Hello, Hugo! I thought we should hear from you sooner than this," Aunt Dorothy exclaimed.

"You would have," he said, "but I was warned off," and he looked at Harry.

Aunt Dorothy said, "Oh!" in a very cold and disagreeable voice, and added:

"Is that true, Harry?"

"I don't know what you are talking about," Harry answered in a tone of voice which showed he did really.

He plunged into a long conversation with Baba, who looked at Aunt Dorothy under her eyelashes in a most cat-like way.

Lord Hugo walked over to me and said:

"Well, Maxine, how are you enjoying London?"

"Most awfully," I replied—"every moment of it!"

"Will you come and dine with me tomorrow night?" he asked.

But I said I was sorry, I was afraid Aunt Dorothy had planned something else.

"I have planned nothing," Aunt Dorothy said. "Why not go, Maxine? You will enjoy yourself."

She said it in such a snappy way, as if she was paying me out for something, and I could not quite see why, as she must have known perfectly well I did not want to go with Lord Hugo.

I was just feeling desperate, and wondering how I could possibly say I could not go, when Timmy said:

"Too late, Hugo. Maxine has promised to dine with me—haven't you, Maxine?"

He winked at me, and I said:

"Yes, so I had."

Lord Hugo must have guessed it was a put-up job, but he did not seem to mind a bit, and just said:

"Well, when can I see you?"

"Perhaps you will telephone," I answered, thinking it would be easier to put him off then.

It was terribly nice of Timmy to rescue me. I do think Lord Hugo is a horrible old man.

REFLECTION SIX

I have been kissed for the first time, and I am terribly disappointed.

I had always looked forward to my first kiss, or, anyway, to being kissed, thinking it would be tremendously exciting, and now it has happened I just feel frightfully disappointed.

Just before it happened I was rather thrilled, and yet had a sort of sinking feeling inside, as if I was going to be sick.

Then it seemed a frightful anti-climax, and really I cannot think why people make such a fuss about flirting, if that is all there is to it.

I went out with Timmy. He called for me about nine o'clock, and I wore one of my very newest dresses—a green lace, which I think looks awfully nice with my hair. So did Mabel, because she said:

"Well, if you're not a success to-night, Miss Maxine, you ought to be—that's all I can say."

"I hope I am, Mabel," I said, and she asked me whom I was going out with.

When I told her I was going out with Lord Weatherley, she said, "Oh him!" most disappointedly.

"Why 'Oh him!' Mabel?" I said. "Do you not like Lord Weatherley?"

Mabel said he was all right, but had been hanging about for years, and then Aunt Dorothy came in, so I could not ask her any more.

We dined at a funny little place in Dover Street, which was very quiet, and Timmy asked me all about myself.

I told him about the convent, and about Mummy, and he seemed frightfully interested.

I had some champagne to drink, but only a very little, because I do not like it much; but Timmy said it was very good, and he had some very special brandy after it.

Then he said:

"Where shall we go now?"

I said I didn't care. I thought all the places were most amusing.

He said I wouldn't think that long, or, if I did, I wouldn't say so.

So we went to the Embassy again, because he said everyone would be there, and we found the same crowds as usual. They all rushed up, and the men, I must say, paid me lovely compliments, and said how lucky Timmy was.

But the women kept on saying, "Oh, Timmy—at it again!" which seemed to me a very silly expression, and quite irrelevant.

We danced for some time, and then we talked some more, and then Timmy said:

"I have got the most lovely new American records at my flat that I would love to show you."

I said perhaps I could come and hear them some day, and he said:

"Why not come now?"

I answered I thought Aunt Dorothy would not like me to go to a man's flat at that time of night, but he said that would be quite all right as his sister Kitty was staying with him.

So I said, "All right," and we went off to his flat, which I think was in Davies Street.

It was a lovely flat, awfully expensively furnished, and the walls were of pine panelling. He had huge armchairs, and a great big sofa covered with cushions.

Just before we got to the flat, I asked was his sister there, and he said, "Oh, yes," but when we got upstairs the whole place was in darkness, and I said:

"It does not look as though your sister is in."

"Perhaps she has gone to bed," he said. "Don't let us disturb her."

So we went very quietly into the sitting-room and he turned on the lights, and there was a bottle of champagne and two glasses, and some sandwiches, all waiting.

Timmy insisted on my having some, though I said to him:

"Perhaps your sister is out, as the champagne is un-opened."

"I expect she was not thirsty," he said, "when she came in."

He uncorked the bottle and I had some, though I insist-ed on having only a very little in case he was mistaken and she would come back and want some.

Then I said, "What about the records?" and Timmy re-plied that after all he had forgotten that they were not ar-riving until next day, and I would have to come again to hear them.

He sat down on the sofa, and asked me to sit next to him and tell him more about myself.

I explained there was very little more to tell, I had not done very much in the last few years, and I had told him all I had done.

"Nonsense, there is much more to hear," he said, and he wanted to know what I thought about him.

I said I thought he was very kind, and awfully nice to have saved me from having to go out with Lord Hugo.

We were sitting on the big sofa in front of the fire, and he said, "I do adore the colour of your hair, Maxine," and touched it.

I said I was glad he liked it, but I hated people touching my hair—it made me feel like a cat being stroked the wrong way.

Timmy laughed, and answered:

"But I would like to stroke you, Maxine" and I said I should hate it.

Then he looked at me in such a funny way, rather strangely and seriously.

I felt as if something was wrong and I got up quickly and said I must be going home.

"Not yet," he said.

"Yes, please, because I am tired," I insisted and started to put on my cloak again.

As he was helping me, he suddenly put his arms round me and held me very tight, and then I knew he was going to kiss me.

Somehow I did not particularly want to stop him.

I felt frightfully excited and rather strange, and then he kissed me—and I did not enjoy it very much.

It was awfully disappointing. It was a long, long kiss, and I thought he was never going to stop, and when at last he did, I pushed him away, and said:

"Now I must go."

"Darling," he said, in a funny, thick sort of voice, "do not go away," and he reached out to stop me.

But I said, "I must . . . I must," and opened the door of the flat and ran out on to the stairs.

He stood in the doorway, and said:

"Please, Maxine—just a moment more!"

"No . . . no!" I said, and then I remembered his sister, and added, "Hush! You will wake your sister."

"No, I shall not," he said, rather crossly, and put on his coat and came downstairs with me.

He said, "I will get a taxi," but I said, "No," because I felt that in the taxi he would try to kiss me again, and, after all, Aunt Dorothy's house was only just round the corner.

So we walked, and when we got there he said:

"Can I come in for a moment? I want a drink."

I said I was very sorry, but I did not think there would be any, and anyhow, he had not far to go to get back to his own drink!

"You are very unkind to me, Maxine," Timmy said.

I felt quite horrid, as he had been so nice in saving me from Lord Hugo.

"I am not," I said, "I am just sleepy."

"You will be kinder another night, will you?" he asked, and I said, "Perhaps", and went quickly inside before he could say any more.

I am not sleepy, and will not sleep for hours. I do wish I had enjoyed my first kiss more. It was all rather disappointing.

REFLECTION SEVEN

I have had such a thrilling afternoon.

Aunt Dorothy said this morning she was going to have her hair permanently waved, and I must amuse myself for the rest of the day, so we had an early lunch at Grosvenor Square and she went off to the hairdresser's.

I took Lulu, the Pekinese, and went for a walk in the Park.

I do like the London parks, especially when they are all blue and hazy, like they are on a dull afternoon, all the chimneys and towers rising above the trees in the distance like Eastern minarets, and the flowers just big splashes of colour on the green grass.

I walked right up to the Serpentine with Lulu, and threw sticks for him to swim to, but he is an overfed, lazy dog, and he refused to go in.

Then we walked along, and it was still quite early, so I sat down under one of the big trees, and Lulu played with a ball, while I just watched the pigeons, who were much too fat, and the people walking up and down.

It was then I heard a sob just to the right of me.

I looked round the corner of the tree, and there was a woman sitting by herself on the other side, and crying fearfully into a rather dirty pocket-handkerchief.

Her clothes were very shabby, and her shoes were cracked and split.

I was just wondering if I should speak to her and ask her what was the matter, when the ticket collector came up for the money.

I paid my twopence, and then when he said to the woman, "Twopence, please," she jumped to her feet quickly, and said:

"I'm sorry . . . I haven't any money."

"Well, you shouldn't be sitting on this chair, then," he said angrily.

So I turned and said:

"It is all right, this lady is with me," and handed him another twopence.

He looked disagreeably at her, and muttered something about, "You won't have so much luck another time," and then clipped the ticket and walked away.

She wiped her eyes, and said:

"Thank you so much," and sat down again.

"What is the matter?" I asked.

"I don't want to bother you with my troubles," she said.

She talked very nicely, though her clothes were frightfully poor, as though she was really quite a respectable person.

"Please tell me," I said, "I hate to see people unhappy."

I moved my chair a little nearer to hers.

"Well, I can't get a job," she said. "I've been trying for months, and now I've got nowhere to go. I've been turned out of my lodgings this morning."

I asked her what her job was, and she said she was a lady's maid.

I asked her how she had lost her last job, and for a moment she would not speak, and then she said:

"The lady got angry because I burnt a hole in her dress, and turned me off without a reference. The Registry offices are overcrowded with people nowadays, especially servants, and I can't get work of any sort. I was with her for two years. You see, being turned off like that looks bad against anyone, if they won't give a reference."

I asked her who the lady was, and to my great surprise she said it was Lady Yardleigh, for of course that is Baba, and I do think it perfectly frightful of her to have treated her maid like that. I did not say I knew her, I merely said:

"Surely she could not have turned you off entirely because of that?"

"Oh, yes," she replied.

She told me Baba was noted for being unkind to her servants, but that she had always tried to please her, and had really thought she was settled at last.

I was so awfully sorry for the poor woman. I asked her name, and she said, "Eleanor Denton," and I said:

"Well, look here—let me try and get you some place to go to."

"I will do anything if only I can get work," she said, "but I've got nowhere to go to-night, and the landlady won't let me take my box away."

She started to cry again.

"Do stop crying," I said. "I will go and talk to my uncle, and see what he can do. As a matter of fact, I know Lady Yardleigh."

"Oh, miss, if only you would, I should be so grateful," she said. "You can ask Lady Yardleigh about me, and though she won't give me a reference, she can't say anything else against me."

So I told Eleanor to come and see me at six o'clock, when I knew Uncle Lionel would be back and I started to walk home.

Who should I meet but Harry, and so I told him all about it.

He said he thought it was horrible of Baba, but it all came of being in the chorus, and knowing no better.

"Who was in the chorus?" I asked.

"Baba was once," he answered, "but she always tries to forget it now, or, if she remembers, tries to pretend she had a leading part."

He laughed:

"The only leading part she has ever had is leading poor old Derek about by the nose!"

Then Harry asked me if I had had any tea, and when I said no, he said:

"Come and have tea with me at Rumpelmayer's—it is always the correct thing to do when you are very young, and I have not done it for years!" I said I would love to,

37

and we went off to the shop in St. James's, which of course I had always heard about, and had masses and masses of cakes, which made me feel very stuffed and fat, but they were very good.

The bill was enormous, and I thanked Harry and said I was sorry I had been so expensive.

He laughed and said:

"If you are never more expensive than that, no one will mind! But I am sure you will be."

"Why?" I asked.

"There is no need for me to tell you that, Maxine," he replied. "I am sure Hugo and Timothy have said it beautifully."

"Said what?" I asked, rather mystified.

Because Harry and Aunt Dorothy and all that crowd always talk with a sort of underlying meaning to their sentences, which I seldom understand, and which becomes very annoying after a time.

"Oh, do not fence, Maxine!" answered Harry. "You know you are attractive, or, anyway, you ought to by this time."

I said I did hope that I was, because I thought that already Aunt Dorothy was getting rather tired of chaperoning me.

Harry laughed.

"Hardly her job, all that, is it?"

I said no, I supposed she was frightfully young to have the bother of chaperoning a girl. He laughed again, but not in a very nice way, and said he was not exactly referring to age.

Anyway, we left it at that, and when I got home I rushed to Uncle Lionel, who had just come back from the House, and told him about Eleanor.

He said if I liked I could have her as my own maid, which was perfectly wonderful of him, and I was so frightfully pleased, because, apart from being sorry for her, it will be fun to have a maid of my own.

I thanked him and gave him a kiss, and he said:

"There, there, Maxine—if you become so excited over such a small thing as a maid what will you do when someone gives you a pearl necklace?"

38

I said I was not certain that I would not rather, at the moment, have a maid and he said:

"Long may you think so, my dear."

He gave me some money to give Eleanor to get her box and some new clothes.

When she came, she was absolutely thrilled, and then burst into tears again, and said she would work her fingers to the bone for me.

I do hate people crying, so I just begged her to stop doing so if she wanted to please me. So she tried awfully hard, and said she would come that very night, and I rushed off to tell the housekeeper.

So now I am very smart, with a maid of my own and I do think that Harry was terribly nice.

I am sure it would be more amusing to kiss him.

REFLECTION EIGHT

I still think it would be very interesting to kiss Harry. I wonder if I ever shall?

I know Mona said that he did not like girls, and I suppose he is only being kind to me to please Aunt Dorothy. Not that it always seems to please her as much as it did— in fact if he talks to me very much she gets annoyed.

But that may be because she thinks I am bothering him; and after all—as he is such a 'catch'—if he got bored he need not come to the house any more.

We have got a party to-night. It is half-way through now, and I am here in my bedroom for just two minutes to get away from everybody.

The evening started with a large dinner-party, with lots and lots of people, and then we went up to the ballroom where a band had arrived.

Everyone danced, and there was an oyster bar and lots of drinks. Heaps of people came in afterwards, until the room was quite packed and it was almost impossible to move.

A good many people, thinking there was not room, went and sat out in all the bedrooms, and when I ran upstairs here an hour ago to powder my nose, I found two people lying on the bed in the dark.

They said, "Oh!" when I went in, and sat up hurriedly, and I do think it was rather a cheek.

Anyway, they did not seem to mind my coming in, or be a bit embarrassed!

They lay back again and said:

"Your bed is very comfortable, and we are absolutely exhausted."

"Why do you not go home if you are so tired?" I asked.

After that they did not answer, or speak to me.

When I went out, I left the door open and the lights on, and I heard the woman say:

"Damn the girl! Get up and shut the door."

I really do think some people have no manners at all.

Heaps of people kept disappearing for a long time into different rooms in the house, and I asked Timmy when he danced with me why people sat out so long.

"This is one of Dolly's petting parties," he replied.

I knew what that meant, and I said I thought they only had them in America, and Timmy laughed, and said all nations were much the same!

Anyway, I refused to sit out with anyone, and just danced and danced, because I do like it so much and the band was perfectly marvellous.

Harry danced with me. He was most awfully nice, and he does dance well. He is very tall, although I am not very short I can hardly see over his shoulder when we are dancing, and when Aunt Dorothy is with him she looks more minute than usual.

It was rather hot in the ballroom, and when I had finished one dance with him we went on to the balcony.

"Happy, Maxine?" he asked.

"Terribly!" I answered.

I said it was nothing to do with the life, but I was just happy, and did he never feel happy for no reason at all, like one does on a spring morning when one wakes up, and nothing particular is going to happen, but you feel as if it might.

"Yes," he said. "I feel like that in Scotland."

I said I would adore to go to Scotland because I had never been.

"One day I will take you," he said.

"Will you really?" I asked.

41

"Of course, if you will come with me," he replied. "Will you?"

"How perfectly marvellous!" I said. "When?"

He leant forward and took my hand in his, and was just going to say something frightfully interesting, when Aunt Dorothy appeared in the window.

"Harry," she said in a sharp, rather crisp voice, "I want you to come and help me arrange about the Cabaret turn."

"Oh," he said, "will it not do in a moment or two?"

"No . . . at once," she replied.

Then she saw who was with him, and she said:

"Maxine, I want you to meet Lord Rosdean."

And she introduced me to a tall, rather vacant-looking youth, who came out and sat on the balcony with me and talked the most awful nonsense I have ever heard.

He talked and talked, and I was frightfully bored, and somehow suddenly I did not feel happy any longer; I did not quite know why, but the party did not seem so amusing as it had before.

Anyway, we sat and talked for twenty minutes until the band came back, and I could not help thinking how much more interesting it would have been if I could have had that twenty minutes with Harry.

But he was talking to Aunt Dorothy—at least, she was talking to him. She looked angry, and he looked more indifferent and aloof than usual.

I do think he is terribly attractive, but I wonder why Aunt Dorothy is always making him do things he doesn't want to do.

At last I could stand Lord Rosdean no longer, and I said, "Let's have a drink," and we went into the bar, and there was Baba standing by Derek. I said to her:

"Oh, Lady Yardleigh—I have got your old maid,"

"Who? Eleanor Denton?" Baba asked.

"Yes," I answered.

"My dear, she is the most frightful woman!" said Baba. "She absolutely ruined a dress of mine, and so I sent her away without a character. I do advise you not to have her."

"Thank you," I said, "but I have already engaged her.

She was starving because you would not give her a character."

"But I do think one ought to be absolutely honest about one's servants," said Baba. "I think it is really dishonest to give a character to a servant who is not worth it. You do agree with me, don't you, Derek?"

Derek muttered something, but I do not think he really agreed with her, and she said:

"Does Dorothy know you are having this woman, Maxine?"

I told her Uncle Lionel had said I might have her.

"Well, I think I had better tell the old boy," Baba said.

"Do," I replied, "but he knows the story already, and has also given me permission to have her."

"Well," said Baba, "be it on your own head, but if your clothes are ruined, do not blame me!"

I said that I would not, rather coldly, because I do think she is a cruel and unkind woman.

Then the band started, and when we all got back to the ballroom there was a roll of drums, and we had a cabaret.

There was a most awfully funny man, who dressed up in a wig and shawls and sang songs which apparently had double meanings in every line. I must say I did not understand half of them, but everyone else screamed with laughter, and encored and encored.

When that was over, Harry came straight up to me and said:

"Can I have this dance?"

Of course I said yes, and then that fool Lord Rosdean said:

"Oh, but this is the end of my dance—we only had two turns before the cabaret."

Aunt Dorothy was just behind and heard what he said.

"Of course, Maxine," she said, "you must not be rude and cut dances at your age. Harry can dance with me."

"Oh, I do not think I will bother," said Harry. "I will have a cigarette outside."

Aunt Dorothy went quite pink, and said:

"I want to dance with you, Harry."

"Oh, very well then," he said, and danced, with what I thought was very bad grace.

43

Lord Rosdean turned to me with an inane smile, and said:

"You seem to be causing trouble in the camp!"

"What camp?" I said coldly, because I did not want to dance with him—I thought he was so stupid!

"You will have to learn not to poach on other people's preserves," he said, "or you will cause a great deal of trouble."

I said I really did not know what he was talking about, and would he put it in plain English.

"Oh, well," he said, "if you must have it, Harry Standish belongs to Dolly, and it is no use you butting in."

I said how could he belong to Aunt Dorothy when she was married? He roared with laughter and did not answer.

On thinking it over, I think perhaps I see the whole thing. Aunt Dorothy is in love with Harry, and I am awfully sorry for poor Uncle Lionel, who is such a darling.

I think it is very naughty of Harry, but I must say he does not look as if he is very in love with Aunt Dorothy.

Perhaps he is not really. Perhaps it is only she who is in love with him, for she must be years and years older than he is.

Anyway, I hate them all, and I do not think it is a very happy ending. No—that is not true! I do not really hate Harry. He is quite the nicest person I have met in London.

I can hear the band—I must go down. I am enjoying myself—I am really.

What a little beast I am to find fault!

REFLECTION NINE

I love Harry . . . I do terribly.

And I think . . . I am not sure . . . but I think he loves me!

The party went on and on. It got later and later, for no one seemed to think of going home.

Having once got introduced to Lord Rosdean I could not get rid of him. He hung about, trying to dance with me, dance after dance, till in the end I said:

"Oh, do let me dance with someone else!"

I do want to get to know a lot of people before I decide on any one person.

He rather grumbled, but went away to dance with Mona and some of the other girls, who all seemed to be enjoying themselves frightfully.

Having got rid of him, I was just looking round—and I must own, if I am to be quite truthful, that I was looking for Harry—when who should come rushing upstairs but Lord Hugo.

He never even asked, but seized me round the waist and whirled me into the middle of the floor.

"At last we have another dance together, beautiful one!" he said.

"You should ask first, surely," I replied.

"Oh no," he answered, "I have learned never to do that—because you might have said no.

"You are so sweet," he continued the next moment. "Do you know what I want to do?"

I said, "No" rather coldly, not really listening, because I was trying not to dance as closely as he wanted me to.

I do hate being crushed, and he was ruining my new frock, which was of green tulle.

"I want to kiss you!"

"No . . . certainly not!" I cried.

"Do not be so horrid!" he said.

"It is not horrid not to want to kiss somebody, is it?" I asked.

He said yes, he thought it was.

We danced on and on.

Presently he suggested:

"Let us go down and have some supper."

I was so glad of an excuse not to dance with him any more that I said:

"All right, let us."

We went downstairs.

The supper-room was full at the moment, and so we went to wait in the smoking-room, which adjoined it.

The room looked right into a long, private garden at the back and Lord Hugo said, "We must get some air"—as it was so hot.

The garden was all lit with fairy lights, and little seats had been put everywhere, so we walked out there.

There were lots of people sitting on the seats, so I thought it would not matter.

But at the end of the garden there were some huge screens of flowers and an empty seat, on which Lord Hugo sat down, saying:

"Better rest a few moments, and then there will be sure to be a place for supper."

I sat down beside him, and at first he talked quite nicely, only he kept paying me rather stupid and fulsome compliments.

Then he talked about other things, and was really quite interesting, so I did not notice that the people who were sitting in the garden had gone in to dance the next dance.

46

Then suddenly he put his arm round my waist, and said:

"Now be a little nice to me," and pulled me closer to him.

"No . . . please do not do that," I said, and put my hands against his shoulders and tried to push him away.

His eyes were all swimmy and horrible, and I suddenly hated him intensely, but he was awfully strong and pulled me closer and closer.

He put his other arm round me, and I said, " No. . . please," but he bent his head quickly and tried to kiss me.

I dodged it just in time—he only kissed the back of my ear.

I was perfectly furious, because I think he is a horrible old man, and I had showed him I disliked him the whole time.

So I jumped to my feet, absolutely wrenched myself from him, and ran quickly into the house. There in the smoking-room, alone, lighting a cigarette, was Harry.

I do not know why, but I had never felt so upset and miserable, and I rushed up to him and said:

"Oh, take me away . . . please take me away, Harry!"

"What is the matter, child?" he asked.

"That horrible old man!" I said.

He suddenly looked frightfully cross, and said:

"What has the swine been doing to you?"

"Come away . . . come away," I said. "Do not let us argue"—for I saw Lord Hugo coming down the garden towards us.

I do not quite know how it happened, but somehow we rushed outside the front door and got into Harry's car, which was there, and we were rushing through the square, the wind blowing in my hair, and I felt awfully safe and happy.

We drove right up to Hampstead, on to the heath.

It was absolutely quiet up there, and there was nobody about as it was very late.

There was no moon, but only a lot of stars shining on the water and over the trees, and we might have been miles and miles away in the country instead of in London.

Harry pulled up and said:

"I think I will light a cigarette."

"Yes, do," I answered.

"You don't smoke, do you?" he asked.

"No," I replied.

"I am glad," he said.

"Why? Do you not like women who smoke?" I asked.

"Oh, I do not mind as a rule," he answered, "but I think it would spoil you."

I said, if he thought that, I was awfully glad I did not smoke, and he said:

"Do you mean that, Maxine? Does it matter what I think?"

I said I wanted him to think I was awfully nice.

"Why should you want that?" he asked.

I said I did not know, except that I thought he was awfully nice.

When I said that, he said, "Oh, God!" in a funny tone of voice, and threw away his cigarette, though he had only had two or three puffs.

He started up the car, and we drove home fearfully quickly.

He never spoke a word, and somehow I could not think of anything to say.

I wondered if he was cross, yet I did not think he was. I tried hard, but still I could not think of anything to say, and the wind was blowing in my face.

When we got back to Grosvenor Square, there were still sounds of the band, and we could see people dancing through the open windows.

He stopped and parked the car on the other side of the road. Then he turned to me and said:

"Do you feel better now?"

"Yes, much better, thank you."

Then he gave a sort of groan and said, "Oh, Maxine!" and put his arm round my shoulders and kissed me.

It was quite, quite wonderful, and completely different from the other kiss Timmy had given me.

Before I could say anything, before I even realised what had happened, he had opened the door of the car and we were both on the pavement and back in the house.

Everyone was dancing and laughing, and I still did not quite know what was happening, but I found myself dancing with Lord Rosdean again.

I do not know what he said, or if I answered him at all, but as soon as I could I slipped upstairs to my bedroom, which luckily was empty, and I locked the door and got into bed.

And here I am, thinking about Harry and that wonderful, wonderful kiss!

REFLECTION TEN

Harry has not been near me; he has not even been in the house. I have waited in all day, hoping he would ring up.

Each time the telephone has rung I have listened, but it has never been for me, always for Aunt Dorothy. And then at last Newman, the butler, said:

"You're wanted on the 'phone, miss."

I could not even wait to ask who it was.

I just said, "Oh!" and fled into the boudoir, where I knew that I could talk in peace.

I shut the door, and then turned to the writing-desk, and I just waited one delicious moment before I took the receiver off.

It is such a lovely feeling just before you are going to hear something absolutely marvellous.

And then I said, "Hello!" and a voice replied, "Hullo—is that you, Maxine?" . . .

It was Timmy. I could have cried with disappointment.

"Oh . . . oh, it is you!" I said.

"You sound disappointed," he said. "Are you?"

Of course I had to say, "No . . . no," but I was, frightfully. I did so hope it was Harry.

"Can you dine to-night?" he said.

"Oh, all right," I replied, for it seemed that Harry really was not going to ring up.

It was seven o'clock, and the day had been awful, just waiting in the house and listening to Aunt Dorothy complaining about the mess her party had left behind.

All the servants were cross, because they were so tired, and Uncle Lionel had not come home.

So I said yes, and he said he would call for me in an hour.

"Wear your best," he said, "and we will try and wake up everybody!"

I said, "All right," and went upstairs to dress, but even then I was listening for the telephone, for if it rings very loud I can hear a faint buzz even in my bedroom.

But it never rang at all, and Aunt Dorothy had gone to bed because she felt tired.

Eleanor helped me to dress, and I could not resist saying to her:

"Do you know if Sir Harry Standish has rung up to-day?"

"No, miss, I don't think so," she said, "but I can find out."

But I said it did not matter, and just went on feeling desperate.

I put on my dullest dress, the one I liked least, but all my clothes are so lovely that it very nearly had the effect of cheering me up a little bit.

Timmy called for me in frightfully good spirits, and said he had collected a most amusing party, and we were going to all sorts of places.

The party was really great fun, and if I had only been feeling a little more cheerful I should have enjoyed it frightfully.

But I kept wondering why Harry had not rung up.

I could not believe that he had really forgotten all about me, and I did want to speak to him, after last night.

Then I thought to myself that perhaps my kiss had meant as little to him as Timmy's had to me, and it all seemed frightfully difficult and depressing.

Timmy said, "Have a drink—cheer up!" and I had two cocktails, and then lots of champagne, and I really did not seem to mind things so much.

We went to several clubs, and then on to the most extraordinary place called the 'Blue Lamp Club', which was all done up with red, and steel chairs, against white concrete walls.

The only decoration on the walls was a huge fresco of a naked man and woman, and everyone kept saying how thrilling it was to be there, and how they ought not to have come.

I could not quite see why, for it seemed to me frightfully dull.

The band was good, but the women were all in tweedish clothes, mostly with berets on very straight hair, and hardly made up at all.

They seemed to take no interest in the men, who were quite amusing, for they had absolutely fantastic clothes—red or black shirts, and yellow spotted ties.

One who was in evening dress had a huge orchid in his button-hole, and the most lovely jewelled ring. But they all seemed a little sad, and rather languid—not half as gay as some of the other places I had been to in London.

Anyway, we all danced, and our party kept saying:

"Ooh—look at that one! ... Darling, I am being a success to-night!"

The most extraordinary-looking man, with an eyeglass and a green shirt striped with red, came over to Timmy and they all said:

"Timmy has got off!"

I suppose he must have asked Timmy if he might introduce him to one of the strange women in tweeds.

Anyway, Timmy said no, and got up and danced with me.

There were more drinks, but the place was so odd I really could not bear it, and so I asked Timmy if we could go.

"Of course," he said. "Let's go to John's party."

"Who is John?" I asked, and said I did not know he was giving a party.

"Every Wednesday night," they all cried, "but we have all got to take a bottle."

So we bought three bottles of whisky from the bar and jumped into a taxi—eight of us in one taxi, such a crowd! And we went off to where John lived.

52

It was apparently an attic, but he had made it awfully attractive by painting all the walls bright red, with black patent-leather curtains.

We all sat about on the floor, and drank all sorts of peculiar drinks, especially a hot punch, which apparently was made up of a little bit of every drink we had brought.

The gramophone played wild music, and everybody talked about the most extraordinary things—at least I thought they were extraordinary, and did not quite understand what everyone meant.

But it was all awfully clever and intellectual for a little while, and then two or three men got up and did impromptu cabaret turns.

One man with a banjo was awfully good—the rest were rather silly, I thought.

It all became rather hazy, because Timmy kept getting me glasses of hot punch, and though it tasted awfully good it made me terribly sleepy.

At last Timmy said, "Come on—let us go home, Maxine," and when we got into the taxi I found that he and I were alone together.

I felt so sleepy that I put my head against his shoulder, and he kissed me again and I did not stop him, because I was so frightfully tired.

Then suddenly the taxi stopped, and I looked out and saw we were at Davies Street.

"No, Timmy . . . I want to go home," I said.

"Just for a moment, Maxine—do!" he begged.

I said no, and he said, "Please!" and started to kiss me again, and I suddenly thought how perfectly horrible it was, and that I hated him kissing me.

His hand was stroking my bare arm, and I said, "No . . . no, Timmy!" and tried to push him away.

He said, "Do not be silly," and kissed me harder than ever, and it was all horrible!

At last I pushed him away with all my force and said:

"Please take me home at once."

I think I started to cry—it had been such a miserable day, and I was so depressed inside me about Harry.

He stopped then, and said, "Poor Maxine! I am a brute, aren't I?" and told the taxi-man where to go.

"I am sorry, Maxine. Do not cry, please," he begged.

I pulled myself together just as we arrived at Grosvenor Square and got out and said:

"Good night, Timmy."

He told me he would ring me up in the morning, and told me not to be unhappy.

I let myself in with a latchkey, and the house was absolutely quiet. For once I did not go up in the lift, but started to walk up the stairs.

As I got to the first floor I heard someone opening a door on the floor above, and I thought:

"That is Aunt Dorothy, how awful! I cannot see her. I have been crying, and she will want endless explanations."

So I stood quite still, and then, as someone moved, I crept back into the shadow of the alcove where there is a statue, just before one goes into the drawing room.

And then suddenly on the floor above me a light shone from an open door, and I saw Aunt Dorothy standing there in her long white velvet dressing-gown edged with sable.

And there was a man with her, but for a moment I could not see him, and then I heard her say in almost a whisper:

"Darling . . . you need not go yet! It is quite early."

"I must. Do be careful—someone will hear you," he answered.

With that he turned and walked quickly down the stairs.

And I stood absolutely still, too stunned even to think . . . for as he passed me I saw it was Harry.

REFLECTION ELEVEN

I cannot formulate my own thoughts, I can hardly think coherently at all, and yet of course I now understand.

How stupid I have been all along, and how silly everyone must have thought me!

Of course, everybody but me knew that Harry was Aunt Dorothy's lover.

What a funny word 'lover' is!

We used to talk about them at school, and of course the French girls were always hoping that they would have one as soon as they were grown up, but somehow the word 'lover' got connected in my mind with the first act of 'Rosenkavalier'.

When I thought of a lover I always thought of someone in knee-breeches and their hair tied in a bow.

Now I find that a lover means Harry. It all seems awful, and yet I am trying not to be hysterical and stupid about things.

I have read lots of books about Society, and of course I knew that Society women have lovers. But somehow it is different when you know the people.

I did not expect Aunt Dorothy, because she is my aunt, to be anything but faithful to Uncle Lionel.

It all sounds terribly priggish, and as if I was a perfect

fool. I think that I must have old-fashioned ideas about relations.

I know I was terribly surprised when Mummy said she was going to get married.

I knew she was very pretty, and that heaps of people admired her, but somehow I could not think of her being made love to and living with a man.

It is all so difficult to think out, even to myself. All I can think of now is Harry's face when he kissed me.

What am I to do? How can I possibly face him again now, knowing what I do?

Naturally that kiss did not mean anything to him. How could it, when he is used to somebody as clever and as attractive as Aunt Dorothy?

But, oh, how I wish that he had never kissed me, because then I should have gone on thinking that all kissing was like Timmy's, dull and disappointing.

Instead of which . . .

But I shall not think about it any more. I must try and go to sleep.

REFLECTION TWELVE

I have had an extraordinary day.

Such a lot of things seem to have happened, and I want to get them straight in my own mind.

First of all I could not sleep at all last night, and just lay awake and thought and thought, and the more I thought the more complicated life seemed to be.

One thinks one knows everything, but somehow one does not realise how vague or wrong that knowledge is until things happen.

Then I got up at eight o'clock and had a bath, and I was dressed when Eleanor came to call me at half past nine. She was surprised, but I told her I was going out for the day, and asked her to make some excuse to Aunt Dorothy.

She thought I had an engagement with a young man, so she was frightfully sympathetic and helpful, and I ran downstairs and disappeared out of the house without seeing anybody else.

I had never been out in London so early before. The streets seemed so empty and the air much fresher and brighter.

I walked in the Park for a long time, watching the riders in the Row, and then I thought I saw one of Aunt

Dorothy's friends in the distance, so I hurried away and wandered through Berkeley Square and into Bond Street.

It is only when one is walking in London that one realises how fascinating it is, the houses all different shapes, some of them strange and mysterious looking as if they held all sorts of ancient secrets.

I walked on and on, until I found myself in a funny sort of market, with booths all up a tiny street.

All the people were shouting their wares and tried to make me buy.

"Come and look, dearie—only sixpence, my dear—this'll do you."

But they were awfully nice, and not a bit disagreeable when I said no.

Suddenly I realised that I was very hungry, and when I looked at my watch it was half past one!

I had been walking ever since I left Grosvenor Square, and I looked about for somewhere to eat.

I had lunched out heaps of times in London with Aunt Dorothy and her friends, but always at places like the Ritz or the Carlton, and of course I did not want to go there alone.

I was walking along such funny little streets, and guessed I must be in Soho, because all the shops were Italian or French.

I looked into one or two of the tiny restaurants, but some of them were very crowded, or there was a horrible smell of greasy cooking, and then on the corner of a street I saw one which looked very quiet.

So I walked inside, and an old Italian waiter showed me to a table in a corner.

They were long tables, at which about eight people could sit, but mine was quite empty except for a man at the other end, who was reading a newspaper called 'Advance'.

On the other side of the room there were two women, quite old, but so funnily got up. One was frightfully painted, with blue on her eyelids, and very pink and white cheeks, and the most terrible peroxide hair. The other one had light hair and a magenta-coloured hat, which was a terrible contrast.

They stopped talking when I came in, and stared at me, which made me feel quite embarrassed.

However, the waiter rushed up with the menu, and I ordered myself an omelette, and a small steak.

I felt I could eat everything, I was so hungry!

He asked me what I would like to drink, and I thought it would be most amusing to have some Italian wine, which was absurdly cheap, only one or two shillings.

But when I had ordered it, he said I must pay now, as they had not a licence, and had to send across the road.

I opened my bag, and found that I only had a five-pound note, and when I gave it the waiter seemed quite surprised, and the women whispered to each other.

He took it to the proprietor—a fat, greasy man by the cash desk—and he looked at it too, and I could not help thinking how awful it would be if it was not a good one.

But apparently they were satisfied it was all right, and the waiter went hurrying across the road with it in his hand.

My omelette came quite quickly, and I was glad to see it.

I was just finishing it, when the peroxide woman from the other side walked across and sat down beside me, and said:

"You will pardon my speaking to you, but have you got such a thing as a postage stamp?"

I said no, I was afraid I had not, but probably the waiter could give her one.

She said it did not matter, but she wanted to write to her sister, who was very ill. I murmured vaguely I was sorry and she said yes, so was she.

But she really could not help her sister, who had been dying of pneumonia for weeks and weeks, any more, and she had five children, all of whom were starving.

Then she started to say:

"Would it be too much to ask you to lend me some money to go and see them?"

Before I could say anything, the man at the end of the table put down his paper and said:

"You can cut out that stuff, or I'll have you thrown out."

I had forgotten he was there, and was so surprised when

he spoke, but the woman got up at once and said in the most sarcastic tone of voice:

"So you've been listening, have you? Well, Mr. Nosey Parker, I'll tell you . . ."

"Shut up!" he interrupted. "You heard what I said."

To my surprise, she flounced away, picked up her bag and gloves from the other table, and she and her girl friend walked out, both absolutely furious.

The man turned to me, and said:

"You shouldn't listen to stories like that."

"Was it not true, then . . . about her sister?" I asked.

"Of course not," he said. "She saw you had some money and meant to relieve you of it some way or another."

"Oh!" I said.

Then of course I thanked him for sending her away.

He was rather a strange-looking man, quite young, very dark, with a sort of determined look—I cannot explain it any other way except that he gave the impression he was always just going to fight something or somebody.

When I had finished thanking him he said:

"What are you doing here? Are you looking for a job?"

"No," I replied, "I have only run away from home for the day."

He laughed and said he had done that six years ago, and never gone back yet.

I asked if his people did not mind, and he answered, oh no, he had been cut off with the proverbial shilling. I asked why, and he said:

"Because I had the courage of my own convictions."

After that we began to talk about all sorts of things, and he was really most frightfully interesting.

It appeared that his father and mother were very respectable, and that they considered him a Bolshevik, and he had written a book on 'Progressive Thought', of which they greatly disapproved.

His name was Ivor Vergen—his grandfather had been a Russian.

Then he asked me about my life, and I told him about Aunt Dorothy.

He was frightfully scathing about her—not that he knew her, but about what he called 'that type of living'.

When he started to speak his eyes flashed and the words absolutely rushed from him.

"Take the young men," he said, "what do they do with their lives? Nothing at all. If you ask them what they want to do, they say they want to be happy, and they would like some money. But how do they try to get it? They don't!

"They are just parasites existing on the money their fathers have made before them, with no ambitions, no ideals, and no outlook beyond eating and drinking and women!"

When I thought it over, I really felt that what he said was true, and that we all ought to have something to work for in our lives, and be ambitious for something.

Then he talked about the nation, and politics, and it does seem awful that everything should be in such a bad way, and that no one seems to realise it or do anything about it.

I tried to remember all he said, so that I could ask Uncle Lionel to make a speech in Parliament and tell them how badly the country needed a leader.

When we had sat there for hours and hours, Ivor suddenly said to me:

"Come down to Chelsea with me. I'm going there now, and I'll introduce you to some people who really think. I don't expect you have met many."

I said I would love to, and I paid my bill and was going to tip the waiter two shillings, but he would not hear of it, and made me leave only sixpence, saying I was spoiling the market for other people, and that anyway tipping was a disgraceful class system.

When we got outside, I asked if we should get a taxi, but he said:

"Good heavens, no! We'll take a bus."

So we went on a bus, all the way to Chelsea.

I had never been on one before and I must say it was great fun, though rather slow.

As we went down Piccadilly I could not help looking to see if there was anyone I knew coming out of the Ritz, and I thought what a joke it would be if Aunt Dorothy saw me.

But of course there was no one—there never is when you look for people.

61

We went miles and miles down the King's Road, and then we got off the bus and walked down a side street until we came to some funny, rather dirty little houses.

We went into one of these, and climbed right to the top.

The stairs were very rickety, and I kept tripping over holes in the linoleum, and Ivor laughed and said:

"Anyone could see you are used to marble palaces!"

Then he knocked on a door, and somebody shouted, "Come in!" and we went into the largest sort of attic I have ever seen, with an enormous skylight at the top, which made it very light.

There was a huge man there, with a beard, painting at an easel, and he said:

"Hullo, Ivor—come in. Who's this?"

Ivor introduced me, and the bearded man said:

"Sit down and make yourself comfortable. You will find some coffee by the fire."

Sitting round the fire were another man, and a girl who was called Poppy, very dark, with long plaits of hair coiled round her ears.

They said, "Hallo!" but Ivor did not introduce them to me. He just said:

"This is Maxine, a friend of mine. Give her some coffee."

They poured some coffee out of an enormous tin pot into glasses.

It was very difficult to drink, because the glass got so hot, and I had to wait for ages for mine to cool.

Anyhow, they all started to talk, and the bearded man stopped painting and came over and sat down too.

I could not gather what it was all about, but apparently they were awfully angry about some book which someone had published about Russia.

I could not quite see why they should be so angry, as it was all about Russia, but apparently the man who had written it had broken a promise to them, or forsaken their creed, or something.

Anyway, I could not understand half what they were talking about.

When I had listened for some time, Poppy said:

"Oh, hell, let's have a drink!"

And the bearded man said:

"Nothing doing, Poppy. Haven't a bean till Wednesday."

"I've got sixpence," she said. "Has anybody got anything more?"

I said I had, but Ivor said:

"Nonsense, you're a guest—of course you can't pay!"

"Of course not," they all said—"not the first time you come to us," and I felt quite embarrassed for having offered.

Eventually they found two-and-threepence between them, and the other man, whose name was George, went out to get some drink.

He brought back some gin in a long glass, and they divided it absolutely equally between them all.

I would not have any, as I do not like gin, but had some more coffee instead.

Presently the door opened, and another girl came in; she was awfully pretty, very thin and tall. She rushed in and said:

"I'm absolutely dead! I've had the most awful day!"

"Why?" Ivor asked.

"I've had to sit for five hours," she said, "and even then he only gave me six bob, because it was all he had."

"What a rotten shame!" they cried.

I gathered that she was an artist's model.

She used the most extraordinary expressions, which I had never heard before.

At last I said I had better go home.

Poppy asked where I lived, and I answered:

"Grosvenor Square."

"My dear, you're welcome to it," she said.

They all started to talk about the idle rich, and I really felt quite ashamed of being one.

Ivor came down with me after I had said good-bye, and he wanted me to go back in a bus, but I really felt I could not face one alone.

So he found me a taxi and gave me his name and address, in case I wanted to see him again—which, of course, I do, because I think he is awfully nice and very interesting.

"Good-bye, Maxine," he said, "don't get spoilt among the fleshpots!"

I said I would not, and asked him if he would come to lunch one day.

He said nothing would induce him to, but if I would ring him up he would come and fetch me, and we would have a meal in Soho.

I said I would love that, and went off, and got back to find that no one had missed me very much, and that Aunt Dorothy had gone out to dinner.

I had dinner in bed—I was not a bit tired, only I felt I could not face alone the enormous dining-room and a but-ler and footman to wait on me.

I wish now I had stayed with Ivor and his friends.

They seem very interesting, and much more alive than other people I have met, and do not scream with laughter all the time like Aunt Dorothy's crowd.

I suppose Aunt Dorothy is out with Harry. I do not want to think of him.

I have tried not to all day, but I am afraid I shall not be able to stop myself now I am alone again.

REFLECTION THIRTEEN

I have seen Harry, and met him, and managed to say "How do you do?" quite sensibly.

I have tried very hard to avoid him for some days, and managed quite successfully.

Eleanor found out who was to be coming to each meal, and if Harry was to be there, I made an excuse to be out or not to appear.

To-day at lunch there were only six very dull people.

I was talking to them in the drawing-room, and then, just before Newman announced that luncheon was served, the door was flung open and Harry came in.

It was too silly, but I went absolutely crimson, I know, and my heart gave a big jump, and banged inside me in the most extraordinary manner.

He said to Aunt Dorothy:

"Can I come to lunch, Dolly—although you have not asked me?"

"Of course! Darling, I am so glad you have come— what a lovely surprise!" she said in the purry way she talks to him.

She introduced him to everybody, and then he said, "Hullo, Maxine!" and held out his hand, but I pretended I did not see it, and just said:

"How do you do?" and started handing round cigarettes, although most people had one already!

I think he must have realised that something had upset me, although he did not say anything, but kept looking at me throughout luncheon in a funny sort of way.

When he had finished, I felt he was going to try to speak to me, so before anyone left I fled upstairs, put on a hat and coat and got out of the house.

I dare say it was very cowardly to run away, but I simply cannot speak to him naturally, or laugh and joke.

I know that all that has happened has upset me terribly.

In books the heroine always falls in love with a man who is in love with somebody else, but this is rather different. There is something very indecent about loving a man who loves one's aunt.

It would really be very funny if I did not feel so upset about it.

REFLECTION FOURTEEN

I have discovered that it is no use running away from things in life.

They just happen to one, sooner or later, however hard one tries to get away.

When I came in from my walk the house seemed very quiet, so I thought everyone was out, and I would go and write some letters in the morning room.

I opened the door, and who should be there but Harry alone.

"Oh!" I said. "Where is Aunt Dorothy?"

"She has gone to some committee meeting," he said, "and will not be back till after six."

I said "Oh!" again, and started to leave the room, but he stopped me, and said:

"Do not go, Maxine, I want to talk to you."

"Why?" I asked. "There is nothing to talk about, is there?"

"Oh yes, there is," said Harry. "What is the matter with you?"

"Nothing," I said, which must have been very irritating.

I hate people who say 'Nothing' in a repressed tone of voice, when you know perfectly well there is something the matter with them!

But Harry did not look annoyed. He only said gently:

"Tell me, Maxine—are you angry with me for kissing you?"

I said no, but somehow the way he said it, or perhaps because he was talking about kissing me, made me feel all strange and trembly, like I had that night.

"What is it, Maxine?" he said, and he came across and stood quite close to me.

I was terrified that he would try to kiss me again, because I should not have been able to stop him.

Although I think it is hateful to want to kiss a man who belongs to someone else!

"Tell me, Maxine," he said, and we both stood silent, with something sort of electric in the air.

I felt that I wanted to cry, and I wanted so terribly everything to be forgotten except the fact that Harry was with me.

But of course I could not forget it, and suddenly something seemed to snap inside me, and I felt frightfully angry.

I said:

"If you must know, it is because I have found out about you and Aunt Dorothy. I saw you and I do not want to talk about it, or to have anything more to do with you."

Harry went quite white, but he did not say a word, and I went on.

"Perhaps now you will leave me alone."

With that I walked out of the room and slammed the door, but when I got outside I started to cry and cry.

I rushed upstairs and locked myself in my bedroom and cried for simply hours until I was a perfect freak.

I suppose now Harry will never speak to me again, and though I know I have done the right thing, I am utterly miserable.

REFLECTION FIFTEEN

I have seen Ivor again and he has told me the most awful things about all my friends, not actually individually, but as a whole.

Apparently it is the Society of this country which is absolutely ruining the world. I cannot quite see why, but Ivor says so, and of course it is very difficult to judge yourself from an outside point of view.

I asked what we could do to help it, or, rather, what could I do, and then he said a lot of things about reconstructing the world, and elimination of classes, but it all seemed very difficult to start on.

I do not quite see how one can help being born in Mayfair any more than in Whitechapel.

I asked Uncle Lionel about the world, and he said things were in a very bad way. I asked him what Parliament was going to do about it, but he did not seem to have an answer to that.

The trouble seems to be that everyone knows things are bad, but no one can think of any remedy except Ivor, whose idea seems to be that all the aristocracy must be wiped out.

I suppose it is because I am one of them I cannot see that going to a night club and spending money is doing such a frightful amount of harm, because the people who go are giving their money to the poor and not grinding them down as they did in Russia.

But Ivor says they do, though I do not know it, and that England is the only country that has not had a bloody revolution, and that we are due for it soon.

It all seems very depressing, and I asked Derek the other day what would happen if there was a revolution, but Baba interrupted and said:

"I know what I should do."

Everyone asked what, and she said:

"Live with the leader of it!"

"Well," said Aunt Dorothy, "mind you pick the right one."

"Oh, I am very good at that," Baba said and smiled at Derek in the most sickening way.

I have seen Harry twice since the row, and he has not spoken to me at all.

I am miserable about it, and so lonely, because Harry is the only person who is kind to me in this house.

I do not count Uncle Lionel, of course, because he is never here. He is always so busy at the House—at least, I suppose it is the House, only I heard Baba say to Aunt Dorothy the other day:

"Lionel's new bit is lasting quite a time."

"I hope she does," Aunt Dorothy replied. "When there is an interval between them he is quite unbearable."

I know by now that a 'bit' means a girl friend, and I must say I am glad that poor Uncle Lionel has some friends outside, because no one here pays the slightest attention to him.

All the same, it seems very difficult to know whom to believe, and if anybody is really sincere.

Yesterday I went to tea with Mona.

There were two or three other girls there, all *débutantes*, and they talked about everybody in the most extraordinary way.

I must be an awful fool, because though they are the same age as I am, or even younger, they all seem to know far more about life and people than I do.

I even gathered that they knew all about Aunt Dorothy and Harry, but I simply could not discuss that with them. When she saw how I felt, Mona changed the subject.

She asked me if I had been out with Timmy much, and I said not for a week or two.

"Of course he tried to kiss you," she said.

I said no, I did not think so, and she said:

"I bet he took you back to his flat or tried to."

I said he had done that, and she said:

"The old method! He has tried it on with all of us."

"Tried what on?" I asked.

"Getting us to go back to his flat," she answered, "and then making love to us. Did he tell you his sister was there?"

"Yes," I said.

"Even the same story," she said. "Timmy has no imagination."

"Does she really not live there?" I asked.

They all laughed at me, and said:

"Of course not! She never leaves Scotland, but he always tells the story to anyone who will believe it."

Of course I felt very foolish then, but still it is rather difficult to know who to believe, and one cannot go about the world disbelieving everything that is said to one.

Mona and the other girls kept giggling about all the men they knew, and Mona said she had had four proposals that month. Another girl there said that was nothing, she had had the most marvellous letters from some actor—I did not quite catch his name, but they were all awfully impressed.

She read us extracts from the letters, but they all seemed very dull, and anyway I do not think one ought to read one's love letters to other people.

The girls were all thrilled, and then they asked me what success I had had, and of course I said none.

"What about Rosdean?" they said. "He never talks of anybody else. He absolutely adores you."

I said I thought he was frightful, and awfully dull.

"Do not be silly," they said, "you have made a terrific conquest! Zita has been after him for years."

I asked who Zita was, and apparently she is a very beautiful girl, but with no money and not very much position, and she has made up her mind to marry a title.

So I said as far as I was concerned she could have him, and they said:

71

"Do not be absurd. Rossy is absolutely mad about you."

I said rather acidly that I did not like him, and then I got up to go. I do not think girls are very amusing, at least not Mona's collection.

And then, when I got home, I found Rosdean having a cocktail with Aunt Dorothy.

"Talk of the devil . . . !"

After what they had told me I was awfully cold and off-hand, but it did not seem to make any difference.

He chattered away in his inane fashion, and was quite unabashed when I tried to snub him, and of course Aunt Dorothy has asked him to dinner.

I suppose she thinks I like him, and so that means we shall have to go on to dance somewhere afterwards, and I am really fed up with the whole thing.

REFLECTION SIXTEEN

I have had a proposal.

It is really too ludicrous, and, of course, from that fool Rossy!

I am frightfully disappointed, as I thought my first proposal would be something very exciting, but it is not a bit.

I always imagined myself sitting in a conservatory, with the strains of the 'Blue Danube' being played behind me, and somebody incredibly handsome and good-looking asking me to be his wife.

Instead of which the whole thing was rather ridiculous!

We dined at home, and of course Baba and Derek turned up—they seem to dine here every night—and two other people who were not very exciting, and Harry.

Harry does not seem very gay these days, but I do not flatter myself that it is anything to do with me. I think it is because Aunt Dorothy seems rather cross with him about something.

She keeps asking him questions and fussing over him, and then being snappy the next moment. It is as if she wanted him to do something he does not wish to do. I cannot think what it is, but Harry seems upset and rather silent.

He never looks at me, except accidentally as it were, and then he looks quickly away.

Aunt Dorothy took hours dressing, and so everyone had arrived first, and I had to entertain them.

When Harry was announced, I had to say, "Good evening," and he just said, "Good evening," very curtly, and went across and poured himself a cocktail.

Of course, Rossy noticed it, and said to me:

"Have you and Harry had a row?"

"Of course not," I said. "Why should we?"

"Oh," he said, "been warned off the grass, then?"

"I do not know what you mean," I said and tipped his cocktail as I handed it to him so that it went all over his trousers, so that changed the subject.

He is awfully fussy about his clothes, and looks just like a barber's block.

I am glad I paid him out!

He made just as much fuss as if he had been a woman in a new dress, and Newman had to fetch some hot water and a towel to clean up the marks.

He said it was because the alcohol would make the stuff sticky, but I think really he was frightened of it leaving a mark on his immaculate suit.

After dinner we all went on to the Café de Paris, which is a most amusing place, with a balcony round it where people not in evening dress can sit.

I thought I saw Poppy, but I cannot be certain. Anyway, it didn't seem the sort of place that she would be likely to go to.

We danced and danced, but of course Harry never asked me, and, apart from our row, I am rather sorry that I shall not dance with him again.

He is a beautiful dancer, and somehow I would rather dance with him than with anyone else I have ever met.

Perhaps Ivor is right when he says that dancing is only an excuse for sexual satisfaction. He is always saying things like that, and I don't take much notice now.

It may be in this particular case he is right—not that I mean I feel sexual about Harry, except of course he is the only person I have ever enjoyed kissing, but I just feel sort of comfortable and happy when I am with him.

He does not make me feel either that I am a machine prancing round the room, or else indecently 'bodyish', like Lord Hugo and Timmy do.

However, Rossy and I were made to dance together most of the time, and then at last Aunt Dorothy said we would go home, but when we got outside on the pavement Baba and Derek got into their car and offered to give the other couple a lift.

Aunt Dorothy's Hispano came up for her, and Harry said:

"I will walk, Dolly. I feel like getting some night air."

"Oh, Harry," she said, "I want to talk to you."

He said, no, in a very determined way, but she said, "Yes—I insist."

While they were arguing Rossy took me by the arm and jumped me into a taxi before I could say anything, and he gave the address and slammed the door.

"Why," I said, "what are you doing?"

"Do not be silly," he replied. "Did you not see that Dolly wants to be alone with Harry?"

I said it did not look as if Harry wanted to be alone with her—quite cattishly, I thought, for me!

I was really annoyed at having been jumped into a taxi like that with Rossy.

"Oh, do not be silly, Maxine," he repeated, "you really are awfully dense at times. Of course they want to go home together alone, like I want to go home with you."

"Oh, all right," I said. "I did not realise I was being tactless."

Rossy laughed his inane laugh, and said:

"You've been doing nothing else since you came to Grosvenor Square. A most unsettling little person, you are!"

I remembered that was what Tommy said was wrong with my face, and really it seems very unfortunate if everywhere I go I upset and unsettle people.

But I had not time to think about that then because Rossy tried to kiss me.

"No! don't . . . I don't want to be kissed," I said firmly.

"Look here, Maxine," he said, "you have got to marry me."

I was absolutely stunned with surprise, and said:

"Good gracious, no!"

"Of course you're going to," he said. "Don't be so

silly. You know I shall make you very happy, and you are quite the prettiest girl I have seen for years."

"I shall do nothing of the sort," I said.

Then the whole ludicrousness of the situation struck me, because there we were, bumping along in a frightful old taxi, sitting bolt upright side by side, instead of my accepting or refusing the proposal gracefully.

Before I could think, I said:

"Do you know this is my first proposal?"

"Good!" Rossy said. "What could be better? They always say *le premier fois* is the best."

"Well," I said, "it will not be the best for me this time, because I don't love you."

"Do you love anybody else?" he asked.

"No," I replied.

I don't love Harry now. How could I, after all I know about him?

"That is all right then," said Rossy. "I have always been told girls never have much feeling. You will love me in time—I will teach you to."

With that he laughed in a silly way and kissed my hand. I tried to take it away, but he would not let me, and then we got to Grosvenor Square and he said:

"Good-night, Maxine—I will see you to-morrow."

I said, "Good-night," only too thankful to be home, and I ran inside and went up to bed.

I could not help listening to hear Aunt Dorothy's car come back, which it did very shortly afterwards, and then I suddenly thought that perhaps Harry had come back too.

Of course I could not really have heard them going upstairs, but I just put my fingers in my ears and pulled the bedclothes right over my head.

REFLECTION SEVENTEEN

The most frightful thing has happened!

I can hardly bear to think about it, and do not know what on earth to do.

I am absolutely desperate!

If only Mummy was not so far away I would have some-one to turn to.

I had always thought that when one gets into holes it was mainly one's own fault, and one ought not to squeal at the consequences, but it does not seem as though this is my fault, or that I could have prevented what is happening.

Aunt Dorothy insists on my marrying Rossy.

The whole thing is unreal and fantastic, like an awful nightmare, and the more I protest the less people listen to me.

I woke up in the morning, not thinking much about Rossy's proposal of the night before. I thought he quite understood that I had refused him, and I had arranged to ride that morning in the Row.

I had been doing it for the last few mornings—Uncle Lionel said I could if I wanted to, and I love it.

I learnt to ride, of course, with Mummy years ago, in Somerset, and I used to ride in Paris during the summer term, right out at Saint-Cloud.

Anyway, as it was a lovely morning, the horse came round and I rode in the Row. There were very few people about, and I galloped quite hard, and felt much better for the exercise, and some of my worries seemed to evaporate.

When I got home I had a bath, but I had been longer than I thought, and I was late for lunch, so I hurried into my clothes and rushed into the dining-room.

There were about twelve people there, including Harry and Rossy.

"Good morning, Aunt Dorothy," I said, "I am sorry to be late."

She got up and said:

"Oh, my dear child, I am so pleased ... a thousand congratulations!"

"Congratulations, Maxine! We are so pleased to hear," everybody else said.

"Congratulations on what?" I said stupidly, but it took me some time to get myself heard, and Aunt Dorothy said:

"Do not be secretive about it, darling. Rossy has told me all, and of course, I am simply delighted, and you shall be married from here."

"Married!" I cried with a scream. "What do you mean?" and I looked at Rossy who said:

"I told them about our engagement, Maxine—I hope you do not mind."

"There's not any engagement," I said.

"Do not be silly, Maxine," Aunt Dorothy said, "you need not keep it up now. I know you will not want it announced until your mother has heard, but it is only amongst ourselves."

"Mummy will never hear," I said, "because I am *not* engaged."

Aunt Dorothy looked daggers at me, and said:

"We will discuss that afterwards, Maxine, not in front of the servants, please."

So what could I do but sit down and eat my lunch?

But I feel absolutely desperate. Everyone went on talking just as if I had said nothing, and Rossy whispered:

"Do not be a fool! You are going to marry me."

"I am not!" I said in a furious undertone, but he took no notice.

I looked at Harry, but he was talking to Baba, and I felt then how different it would have been if he had said *he* was going to marry me.

Different for me, I mean ... I do not suppose Aunt Dorothy would have been pleased!

But it was no good thinking about that; I had got to settle Rossy.

During lunch I did not speak, but thought of all the things I was going to say to him afterwards for daring to tell Aunt Dorothy I had promised to marry him when I had not.

But when lunch was over Aunt Dorothy said to me:

"Come with me into the little boudoir, Maxine. I want to talk to you for a moment ... I shall not be long," she said to the other people; "there is just a letter I want Maxine to see."

So we went upstairs, and when we got into the room she shut the door, and there was not a letter at all—it was only an excuse to get me there alone.

"Look here, Maxine," she said, "why are you making this silly fuss?"

"I am not going to marry Rosdean," I said. "I told him so last night, and I cannot think how the mistake has occurred. I think he is a horrible young man, and I dislike him intensely."

"Nonsense, Maxine," said Aunt Dorothy, "of course you are going to marry him. It is the most wonderful match. You know his father is the Earl of Baxmouth, and most influential?"

I said I did not care what his father was, I was not going to marry Rossy.

Then she got awfully nasty, and said she was not going to have me playing about with people, and I had obviously said I would marry Rossy, otherwise he would not have thought so.

She said it was very bad for a *débutante* to flirt with a man up to the point when he thought she had accepted him, and then choke him off in a rude way in public, like I had done.

I tried to explain, but she would not listen, and said either I behaved properly or she would write to Mummy at once and tell her how I was behaving in a most disgraceful way, and how I had led on Rossy until he believed himself engaged to me.

"He has told his mother," she added, "and Lady Baxmouth is delighted. She always wanted Rossy to settle down with a nice girl, especially one with money."

I tried to say some more, but Aunt Dorothy would not listen. She just waved all my explanations on one side, and then she said:

"I am very pleased with you, Maxine, but do not go and get hysterical over this. You are a very clever, lucky girl, and I am sure your mother will be delighted."

I said I would write and explain to Mummy what had happened, and how it was a mistake.

"I cabled your mother this morning," Aunt Dorothy said.

At the moment I believed her, but now, thinking it over, I do not believe she had, as she said it in the sort of way as if she wanted to see what effect it would have on me.

I said, very hotly, I would send another cable to contradict it, and she said:

"If you do, you had better go with it, because you cannot stay here and face the scandal."

I said I was sure Mummy would like to have me, and she said:

"Are you certain of that?"

Of course that upset me, because I know Mummy does not want me to go out to her.

She says it is because of the climate, and the inaccessible spot where my stepfather is Governor. But I personally think that they do not particularly want me, they are both so terribly happy by themselves.

And then, while I hesitated, Aunt Dorothy got quite good-tempered again, and said:

"There, Maxine, do not be such a silly little girl! It is all settled, and, anyway, you need not get married just yet."

There really seemed to be nothing more to say, and I was so upset and worried about the whole thing that I let her take me back to the drawing-room where everybody was, and just acquiesced in everything they said.

I heard her telling Baba and Harry that I was upset because I thought it was a secret, "and", she said, quite roguishly, "you know these young things like a clandestine romance."

I did not speak to Rossy, and he was wise enough not to try and talk to me much.

Instead he said he would call for me that night and take me out to dinner, and then, when the others went, Harry said to me:

"I hope you will be very happy, Maxine."

He said it in such a strange tone of voice, and suddenly I wanted to tell him everything and ask him to get me out of it, but of course I could not, so I just said nothing.

He thought I was still angry with him, and just shrugged his shoulders and walked away.

What am I to do?

And here I am, sitting on my bed, trying to think of a solution, trying to find a way out of this awful muddle.

I am absolutely desperate. I wish I could think of a plan.

REFLECTION EIGHTEEN

I think the telephone must have been invented entirely as a kind of lifebuoy.

I was sitting on my bed, feeling utterly miserable when the telephone rang, and when I took it up I heard Ivor's voice, and suddenly it seemed that he must be ringing me up just to be able to deliver me from all my troubles.

I said to him:

"Ivor, listen. I am in the most desperate state. Can you help me? . . . I do not dare talk too much now in case somebody's listening, but I want to run away. Can you help me?"

He said:

"By yourself, or with somebody?"

"Alone, of course," I replied.

"Poor little Maxine," he said, "has it come to that?"

"Yes . . . and I have got to do it now," I said.

He asked me if I had got any money, and I said a little.

"Well, you had better get all you can, then," he said.

I asked if he could find me a room where I could hide.

"So I am to be mixed up in this, am I?" he said. "I shall very likely be taken in charge for kidnapping!"

I said oh no, he would not be because no one would ever find me . . . not, anyhow, for weeks and weeks.

"All right, Maxine," Ivor said. "You had better bring

some clothes with you if you are really going to run away. It is an awful nuisance being without any—I know, because I tried it."

So I said, "All right, I will."

"I'll meet you outside Marble Arch tube station in twenty minutes," he said.

I flung some clothes into a parcel—I did not dare ask for a suitcase.

I took the oldest things I had got, but first of all I rang the bell and asked Eleanor to ask Miss Roberts for some money, as I was going shopping, and she brought me back ten pounds.

And I wrote two notes, one to Aunt Dorothy and one to Rossy.

To Aunt Dorothy I said:

> Dear Aunt Dorothy,—Please do not think me ungrateful for all you have done for me, but I really cannot marry Rossy, and so I have gone away. I shall be quite safe, so please do not try to find me. I will let you know in a few weeks where I am, but in the meantime you must break off my engagement.
>
> Yours, Maxine.

And to Rossy:

> Dear Rossy,—You and Aunt Dorothy will not realise that I mean what I say, that I have no intention of marrying you. Therefore I am going away, so that you will really know it, and cannot produce me as a fiancée.
>
> Yours, Maxine.

I slipped down the backstairs and through the hall, when no one was about, and went off to the tube station.

Just for a moment, in all the crowd of Oxford Street, I could not see Ivor, and was terrified he had failed me. But of course he had not.

There he was, looking awfully interesting in spite of his shabby clothes, and he took my parcel, and we jumped on a bus and we went down to Chelsea.

83

We went to the bearded man's studio again, and waited till Poppy came.

Ivor explained that I had run away, and she was thrilled, and said I could share her room until I could find somewhere else to go.

We sat about and talked, and I really felt awfully happy that I had escaped Rossy.

I cannot help feeling that I do not mind if I never see any of them again, even Harry, because the sooner I forget about him the better.

REFLECTION NINETEEN

Poppy is the most extraordinary person, but really rather interesting.

She has an engaging, childlike way of talking, but what she says is very grown-up and experienced. She is an orphan, and has earned her own living ever since she can remember.

She draws little sketches for some of the newspapers, or does any odd job that brings her in money. She has been all sorts of things—even a waitress in a restaurant, which she says is awful, your feet get so tired standing about.

She has the tiniest room, just off Flood Street, but she has a camp bed which she has allowed me to sleep on.

It is so different from anything I have been used to. There is only one bath in the whole building, of which all the rooms are let out, and it is only allowed to be used twice a week, when the water is heated from the basement below.

We have to pay sixpence then, and put our names down for a time to use it.

All sorts of people live in the building. Poppy seems to know most of them, and always talks when she meets them on the stairs.

Most of them are women, but there are two or three

men who sleep in the very top attics, and make the most awful thumping when they come home late at night.

We have a gas-stove in our room, with a shilling-in-the-slot meter, and it always runs out just before the kettle boils, or very late when we cannot run out and get a shilling change.

I have arranged with Poppy to pay her three shillings a week for sleeping in her room.

She did not want to take anything, but I know how poor she is, and she is awfully kind about sharing anything she has with me.

The awful thing is I do not think she always gets enough to eat. She looks so thin and pale, and the other day, when she came back from trying to sell some sketches in Fleet Street, she very nearly collapsed.

I found she had had nothing all day since the coffee we had made for breakfast.

So now I go out and buy things myself. It is lucky I have still got so much of my money left.

I am going to try and find myself a job, at least Ivor and Poppy are trying for me, but apparently they are awfully few and far between, so I am being very careful with my money in case it is a long time before I get one.

Of course I have not had a word from Aunt Dorothy or anyone, because they do not know where I am, and I do not suppose they want the publicity of advertising for me in the papers or applying to the police.

I am sorry if Uncle Lionel is at all upset, because he was nice. I wish now I had left him a note too telling him not to worry.

About my job—we all had a good talk in the bearded man's studio, which seems to be used as a sort of meeting-ground for all Ivor's friends.

Somebody said:

"Why couldn't Maxine"—they all call me Maxine, of course, and I have no idea what half their surnames are—"why couldn't Maxine go as a model? She's got a lovely figure."

I said I would love to do that, remembering how I had always wanted to sit for Tommy in Paris.

Then one of the girls said:

"Oh, it isn't easy, or fun, I assure you. I was sitting for

an artist the other day, and he was doing some damn silly Academy picture of a nymph sitting by a stream, or something equally Academyish, and he insisted on pouring water over me to get the sparkle, or some such rot. And, my dear, I was absolutely frozen and had rheumatics for ages afterwards."

"Do you mean to say you had not any clothes on?" I asked.

"Of course not!" she said, and added, "You don't suppose anyone wants you to stand in clothes, do you? They can do all that on a dummy. They only pay for the altogether, I assure you."

At that, of course, I said I could not possibly think of being a model, I should hate it, and they all said:

"Oh, but you're not human to an artist. They look upon you entirely as a machine."

But Poppy laughed and said:

"Don't you believe it, Maxine . . . Don't you remember old Akers?" she asked the others, and they said, "Oh, he was a disgusting old man," and started telling the most frightful stories of how he behaved to his models.

That absolutely decided me.

I would rather go back to Grosvenor Square than be a model to some horrible old man who would want to mess about with me.

When I think of horrible old men, I always think of Lord Hugo, and I really could not bear it if I had to work with someone like that.

Anyway, Ivor stuck up for me.

"Of course Maxine can't be a model," he said. "Think of something else, Poppy."

Talking of models reminded me of Tommy and made me ask myself why I had not written to him before, and I mean to sit down and write him a long letter, telling him exactly what has happened.

I feel somehow Tommy will understand.

Perhaps he and Thelma will ask me to go over to Paris and stay with them for a little while, until Aunt Dorothy becomes more sensible.

REFLECTION TWENTY

I have got the most awful cold, and feel terribly ill.

Ivor took me to an extraordinary party two nights ago. It was given in a studio, not like the one I went to with David when I first came out, but a much bigger studio.

The people were quite different, all in rather dirty, untidy-looking clothes, but all very intelligent and clever-looking.

Some of them, I must say, looked as if they could do with a bath, but if they have the difficulties that we have in this house, I do not blame them for not having many.

Anyway, as so often they seem hungry, I do not suppose they want to spend sixpence on a bath.

This studio belonged to two girls who do posters for somebody-or-other's condensed milk. They were awfully nice and gay, and there were heaps of people there.

We sat about and talked, or else listened to a rather noisy gramophone, and there was whisky to drink, in all sorts of odd-shaped glasses, which seemed to have been collected from everyone, but no soda-water, only plain water.

Although I noticed that a lot of people seemed to prefer it neat. And there was coffee and cocoa, and some rather large sandwiches which had come from a restaurant across the road—at least, so somebody said.

The most extraordinary woman came and talked to me for ages.

She was small and dark, and, I think, a Russian, and she said all sorts of nice things to me. She held my hand, and asked me to come and see her. I said I would like to, and then Ivor came up and said:

"Nothing doing, Renée—I'm looking after this child."

"Oh, I'm sorry, Ivor—I didn't know I was trespassing on your property," she said.

"Oh, it's not as bad as all that," he said, "but I think she's a bit young for you."

She laughed quite pleasantly, and said, "O.K. with me!" And when I asked Ivor what he meant, he replied:

"Nothing at all. You will learn quick enough."

"Learn what?" I said—and how could I learn it if there was nothing at all?

"How you ask questions, Maxine," he said.

I answered that he was always talking about finding out the truth and being straightforward and honest with oneself, and how could I be honest and straightforward if I did not know what he was talking about?

I said if there were things I did not know, I thought he ought to tell me.

He said he was not there to be a nurse, and I do think men are too extraordinary, because they always expect you to know everything, and yet if you do not they will not tell you.

I tried to explain it all to Poppy, and asked her what she thought it all meant, and when I started, she said:

"Oh, Renée—she's notorious."

So then I told her what had happened, and she said:

"Oh, I expect Ivor's right—anyway, I'm not going to tell you."

I got quite angry and said I thought it was perfectly beastly of them all to have secrets that I did not know, and she said:

"They are not secrets, my lamb—if they were, you should know them."

Then I told her what I said to Ivor, and how he was always talking about honesty.

"They all talk like that," she answered, "but they like

you really to be an innocent little darling—that's why you're such a success, Maxine."

I replied I did not think I was much of a success with Ivor, he was always talking about world differences or class hatred when I was with him.

Poppy said:

"Oh, don't think Ivor's sexless—he isn't. But you can't expect full-blooded passion on a cup of cocoa and half a sardine."

I said did she really think food made people fall in love more easily, and she said of course it did, and, anyway, it kept them well, and did not make them irritable and disagreeable like starvation did.

She spoke so feelingly that I asked her how she knew, and she said that she had lived with a man once and had been deeply in love with him, and he with her.

But there was the everlasting trouble about money and anxiety about the rent, and no food and no baths.

They fought like cat and dog in the end, and left each other, and she never saw him now, even though she loved him just as much as before.

I think it is terribly sad, and I was frightfully sorry for her, and then I said, rather shyly, in case she was annoyed with me:

"Would it have been better you had married him?"

"Goodness no!" she replied. "He had a wife already!"

I was so surprised, and then I told her a little bit about Harry, and asked her advice.

"Well, it certainly would not bother me," she said, "if I wanted a man, who he lived with. It might be my grandmother for all I'd care!"

I said he had not exactly said he was in love with me, and she said of course that was different and he might really have only been playing about.

But if I really wanted him I ought not to worry what his past has been like, and that people's pasts had nothing to do with their presents.

Why should I be a judge, anyway, having had no temptations?

That did seem to me quite a reasonable point of view, because perhaps Aunt Dorothy did tempt Harry most frightfully.

90

She is very attractive, and most fascinating if she wants to be—especially when she is all dressed up and does not look tired, like she does in the mornings.

"People get all worked up about this sex business," said Poppy. "Don't think I'm saying it isn't important, because it is, frightfully, and anyone who tells you it isn't is a damn liar. But at the same time it can mean very little to either a man or a woman.

"Maybe your Harry was just having a good time with your aunt, and they both know what they're up to, and nobody's hurt.

"If he'd been playing around with a young girl it would be far worse, but, after all, she is a married woman, and ought to be able to look after herself."

I said that even though she was married to Uncle Lionel I thought she was in love with Harry.

"In love my hat!" said Poppy. "I don't suppose she likes him so much that she'd give up her home and her position for him. People who talk about being in love don't know the meaning of the word unless they are prepared to sacrifice a good deal for it.

"Love in real life, Maxine, isn't a Cinderella fairy story. A Prince Charming doesn't pop up under every gooseberry bush.

"And if they do come into your life, I assure you that they are always hampered by wives, or some sort of tie. You are lucky that your man isn't married, like mine was."

I think she is right, and that a lot of our ideas are the fault of all the story-books we are brought up on.

All my life when I have thought about marriage at all I have always planned that I should meet some perfectly marvellous man. That he would want to marry me and I would want to marry him, and everything would be too easy and settled.

But I suppose you cannot have it every way, and now I begin to think about the people I have met none of them seem to have married a Prince Charming and lived happily ever afterwards.

So I suppose that is too much to expect of life, just as Poppy said.

"We're all too greedy, if you think about it. We do expect a lot, and yet we don't want to give much. I know when I lived with Jack I was always wanting him to give me bits of himself, instead of bothering about how much I was giving him.

"It's greed, Maxine, and that always defeats its own end. If I could have my time over again, I should want to make him happy and not keep asking myself if I were.

"I was awfully young, like you, and I thought how much I was doing in living with him when he was married, that I was young and attractive and a virgin.

"I never weighed in the balance that he had experience and brains, and a good deal more charm than I had learned to appreciate at nineteen.

"And now, looking back on things, I'm not surprised that he got tired of me, or that we fought.

"I was quite impossible at times, because of that self-satisfied smugness that insisted that it was I who was doing the generous thing—not he."

We were talking when we were in bed, but Poppy's voice sort of broke on the last words, and I knew that she was crying.

I got up in the dark, and felt my way over to her bed and put my arms round her, and she sort of broke down and said:

"Oh, Maxine, I've been such a damned little fool ... and I am so lonely!"

I could not think of anything to say at all, but just held her very tight, and after a moment or so she pulled herself together and said, in her ordinary, matter-of-fact voice:

"My dear child, you will be frozen! Jump into bed, and forget what I've said."

I kissed her good night, and did as she told me, except the forgetting part. I am going to try to remember that, and I will really strive to be generous-minded.

And now I have got this cold.

Where was I? How did I get it?

We stayed at the party until quite four o'clock in the morning, and then when we came outside it was pouring with rain, and of course there were no taxis.

None of us anyway could afford to take one, so we walked back to our lodgings, Ivor escorting us.

And when we got there we found the landlady, who is a perfect beast, had put the chain on the door.

She hates us being out very late, because she is frightened of burglars, though why there should be burglars in this district I do not know, because as far as I can see there is absolutely nothing worth burgling.

But Mrs. Hopkins—that is her name—always tries to make us all be in by twelve o'clock, and of course to-night we were awfully late, so we rang and banged on the door, but not a sound did we hear.

The rain was pouring down all the time, and we got wetter and my hair was quite soaked and stuck to my face, but still no one came.

At last Poppy said:

"It's no use—she's either dead or drunk. We'd better come to your room, Ivor."

So Ivor said, "All right, come along," and we set off for another five minutes' walk to where Ivor lives.

He has a key, so we let ourselves in and went downstairs instead of up—for he has a tiny room in the basement. Though it is so tiny, it is most amusingly decorated, and Poppy said he'd done it himself.

All the walls were painted with extraordinary pictures, and here and there he'd stuck up a funny futuristic poster and varnished it over.

The effect is very quaint, and he has American cloth curtains, which are very shiny, and hide the one tiny window.

There was a bed in one corner, and a divan in the other, and a chest-of-drawers with a large looking-glass above it.

The nicest thing was a big, darkish carpet on the floor, which I heard afterwards was the one thing he's ever been extravagant about, and had bought at a sale because it had once belonged to Bernard Shaw.

We lit the gas-fire, and tried to dry our clothes, and then Ivor said that Poppy and I had better get some sleep on the bed while he tucked up on the divan.

We took off our dresses and then cuddled close together to try and get warm, but of course my hair was soaking.

We had got chilled right through, and I woke up in the morning with this terrible cold, and now to-day I feel too awful, all aches and pains, and yet very hot, as if I had a temperature.

REFLECTION TWENTY-ONE

Ivor fetched the doctor to me this morning.

He was a charming little man, in a frightful hurry, and not a bit like the doctors I have been used to, with pompous manners and top-hats.

This little man tore in, took my temperature, snapped out several questions which Ivor answered, said I was to stay in bed and keep as warm as possible.

He wrote a prescription quicker than I have seen any-one do, and was gone almost before I realised he had ar-rived!

Apparently nothing very serious—only a bad chill and a sort of influenza on the top of it.

Ivor has been here all day looking after me.

I cannot help being amused to think how shocked the convent would be at the idea of a man sitting on my bed—but no one here seems to think anything of it.

Even Aunt Dorothy's crowd take it quite for granted that your bedroom is a sort of sitting-room.

If Aunt Dorothy was tired, or was going out to a big party, she always lay down before dinner, and if anyone arrived they always had cocktails in her room.

I said once how strange it seemed, after all the fuss the nuns used to make when a doctor came to see one at the convent, and Aunt Dorothy said:

"It is only the middle class who consider bedrooms immoral. It is all on a par with lace curtains and an aspidistra in the window. Immorality should not be connected with where you are, but how you are."

Of course I see that she is quite right, though Baba said:

"That's not an original thought, Dolly—I read it last week in a newspaper."

Poppy is awfully sweet to me, and she has made me some lovely lemonade, because I am so thirsty with this beastly temperature.

I knew she had spent her last penny on the lemons, and had no money for supper, so I said I wanted some sausages, and when they came and she had cooked them I said I really could not eat any.

So of course she then had to finish them up, so as not to waste them, and I had a little Bovril.

I do hope I shall be well soon, otherwise I am afraid my money will run out before I have a job. I have still got about six pounds left, but that is not an awful lot if I have to pay a doctor's bill out of it.

REFLECTION TWENTY-TWO

The doctor came again to-day, and says I am much better.

I have got no temperature, but I feel rather weak and shaky. I am to be allowed to get up to-morrow.

I am glad, because I am awfully tired of staying in this room. I never realised before how dilapidated it is, and I do wish someone would whitewash the ceiling.

I am quite tired of staring at the cracks and stains where the people above have upset water and it has leaked through.

If I ever go back to Grosvenor Square and get some more money I shall make Poppy get a little flat somewhere, and I will pay for it.

I say 'make', but I am not very confident, because Poppy is so independent—I know she hates taking money from anyone—so I will say 'persuade'.

Perhaps if I persuaded her very hard she would have her young man again, and they would live together happily.

Ivor came in before lunch, and back again this afternoon, and Poppy said:

"Will you stay here, Ivor, while I go off and try to sell some drawings?"

She has done some awfully good ones of children playing in the park, with fashionably dressed people looking on—a sort of contrast—and she thought one of the evening papers might take it as a heading to their gossip page.

So she went off, and Ivor sat still and said:

"How shall I amuse you?"

"Talk to me," I said.

"What about?" he asked.

"Oh, anything," I said, "so long as it is not about me. I am rather bored with myself at the moment."

"I can't understand that, Maxine," he said, and smiled.

It was quite the nicest compliment I had ever had paid me, so I smiled too, and suddenly he bent forward and took my hands, and said:

"I love you quite a lot, Maxine. Do you know that?"

I said no, because of course I did not, and he went on:

"Well, I do, but it's hopeless, so there we are."

I suddenly saw how very hopeless it was, because even if I did love Ivor—which I do not—he would never let me use any of my own money, and we could not possibly live together for ever on what he earns.

Of course, he is awfully ambitious, and I feel certain that one day he will get on and be a great man, but he could not possibly be handicapped with a wife, even though he does want looking after.

He ought to have a woman with him to see that he eats enough, and to tidy up the room, which he tries at present to do himself.

"Poor Ivor," I said, "I am sorry about it."

"Sorry be damned, Maxine!" he said roughly.

He dropped on his knees beside my bed and put his arms round me, and kissed me very hard indeed.

It was a rough kiss, quite unlike Harry's or Timmy's, and he seemed rather excited and strange.

I did not feel anything, except very cool and maternal towards him.

I would love to look after Ivor, and try to stop him worrying about all the things in the world which seem to upset him so much.

After all, he cannot stop them, or help them, and it really seems to me a terrible waste, feeling the way he does over world affairs.

I was so sorry for him that I let him go on kissing me.

97

He kept saying, "Maxine! Maxine!" in a strange sort of way, and kissing me harder and harder, with one of his hands gripping my shoulder so tightly that it quite hurt.

At last I said:

"Please, Ivor, don't . . . you are hurting me."

The moment I said that, he let go of me, and dropped his head down on his arms on the bed, and was quite still for some time, and I wondered what he was thinking or feeling.

At last he got up, and I could see his face was very white, and then he walked to the window.

"I'm sorry, Maxine," he said, in a sort of strangled voice.

"Do not be sorry, Ivor, there is nothing to be sorry about," I answered.

Then he gave a little laugh, and said, "Oh, you baby!" and came back and tilted up my chin and kissed me very gently—not in the way he had before.

"Forget it," he said. "Forget everything I said."

"That you love me?" I asked.

"Yes! And don't look so serious about it either," he replied. "It's not as bad as all that."

He sat down on the bed and said:

"I'll tell you something, if you like, Maxine."

"Please do," I answered.

"It's a secret—I've never told anybody. Not even Poppy knows."

"Do tell me, then!"

"As it happens, I'm married," he said.

That was a surprise. I asked him who to, and why?

And he replied:

"When I left home and ran away, I went first of all to live in the north of London. I knew nobody, and I was extraordinarily lonely, but I was working hard on my first book. It was then I met Maureen.

"She was a Chilean, very good-looking in a dark, rather mysterious way. We used to meet and talk about things, and at last I asked her to marry me, and she said of course she would.

"I was very young then, and believed that very soon I should own the whole world, so we got married one spring

98

morning at a register office, and went away on a honeymoon of one night.

"At first we were awfully happy, and then I found that my wife had a good deal more past than I had at first imagined.

"She had all sorts of friends who hadn't appeared before in our brief meetings, which were intervals when I wasn't working on my book.

"They were artists, or people with not much purpose in life. Most of them were foreigners, and pretty soon I began to realise that my wife had lived at one time or another with most of them.

"That didn't worry me particularly, except that she seemed to think she could still be extremely familiar with them, and let them be more or less on the same terms they had been before.

"We had two or three rows about this, and then there was an overwhelming one over a woman called Frances.

"I needn't tell you more about that—sufficient to say that my wife had been a very great friend of hers and had no intention of giving up being her friend because she had married.

"She expected Frances to more or less live with us, and to share her favors equally with me.

"I stuck it for just under a month, and then I walked out and came down here, where nobody knew anything about me, and where I could start again afresh.

"I suffered, because I wanted my wife damnably. I still miss her, but I realise it's hopeless even to try to patch things up. She's not immoral in any way—just totally unmoral, and without any standards at all as regards her affections.

"It didn't matter who or what people were as long as she liked them—and that virtue can be carried too far, as I know only too well.

"There—that's my story," Ivor said. "Not a very exciting one, just rather ordinary, with no finish to it. So you see, Maxine, how things are."

I could not think of anything to say in sympathy, so I just squeezed his hand rather tightly, to show him I understood.

I think he knew what I meant, for he said, "Thank you,

99

Maxine," and then got up and walked about the room as if he were thinking things over.

So everything is just the same between us as it has been before, except that when he came to say good night, with Poppy there, he bent down and kissed me quite naturally, like a brother.

I must say I have grown terribly fond of Ivor, and I should miss him very much if I never saw him again.

There are not a lot of people I would miss, and it's funny, but I keep thinking of Harry and wondering if he has ever noticed I had gone.

Perhaps he just thinks 'Good riddance!'

REFLECTION TWENTY-THREE

I am much better, in fact quite well, and Poppy has found me a job.

I am fearfully excited about it, for it really is a very good thing to get, even though the pay is very small.

There is a funny little antique shop at the top of the road, where a lot of painters sell their pictures, and where one can also buy brushes and paints, as well as lots of real antiques which the owner collects from time to time.

It has an old-fashioned, small-paned glass window, which is generally rather dirty.

The shop is quite tiny, with an old oak counter across the centre of it.

Apparently the man who keeps it is an artist, and he wants someone to mind the shop while he is painting, because he finds it so disturbing to his work to have to answer customers.

He is only prepared to pay fifteen shillings a week, but still that is better than nothing.

He is quite an old man, well over fifty, and he has a room downstairs, built out with a skylight, where he paints.

Apparently he makes quite a lot of money by copying flower pictures and other decorative panels. The shop is amazingly dirty and untidy, even though there are a lot of quite valuable things in it.

But when I offered to tidy it up, he said:

"Certainly not. People who come here think they are getting something really good for their money, and that I don't know the value. Leave it as it is."

There are not many visitors, as it happens, but apparently in a good season a lot of Americans find their way down here, when they are looking at the Bohemian life of Chelsea.

Ivor says the Bohemian life—at least, the sort they are looking for—is all bunkum, and is merely run as propaganda by Cook's, but he is all for it if it brings them to the shop.

Besides my fifteen shillings a week I am to get ten per cent. commission on anything I sell, so I do hope I sell lots and lots, and then perhaps I shall make plenty of money and be able to keep myself entirely.

Now I am earning money I insist on paying a half-share of Poppy's room, as she is quite prepared for me to go on living with her.

That comes to six shillings a week, so I have nine shillings left for my food, although of course there are little extras like the gas-fire and the bath.

Mr. Field, who owns the shop, stared at me in surprise when I arrived this morning.

He had engaged me, of course, on what Poppy had told him, and when I first went in I think he thought I was a customer.

When I explained who I was, he exclaimed:

"Good gracious! I didn't know I was engaging a child of your age."

I said I was quite capable of doing the work, and I hoped I should be able to sell lots of things for him.

He said:

"With that face, you ought to be able to," which I suppose was a compliment.

Anyway, he then went off to his studio, but he came back lots of times in the morning to see how I was getting on, and I was awfully sorry there was not more to tell him than the sale of two paintbrushes and a tube of cobalt blue.

However, in the afternoon a man and a woman came in

and bought a painted box with a Venetian scene lacquered on it, and Mr. Field was awfully pleased, and said I had done splendidly.

I was glad he was pleased, because he must be awfully hard up to be enthusiastic over seven and sixpence.

It was rather boring waiting in the shop all the afternoon, and so few people coming in, and I asked Mr. Field if he would mind my bringing a book the next day.

He said:

"I was wondering if you could help me in my studio. You can always hear the bell if anyone comes in."

I said of course, if I could help, I should be very pleased to be in the studio, and he took me down there, but I did not seem to have very much more to do, except I made him some toast and tea.

But when I left he thanked me again, and insisted on advancing me my first week's wages.

I told Poppy all about my day, and she said:

"M . . . m. Don't let him get too fresh."

"Do you mean that he might try to flirt with me?" I asked.

"I should have thought most men wanted to do that," she said.

When I come to think about it, quite a lot of people have wanted to, so perhaps I have got 'sex-appeal' after all, and I need not wonder any more if I have or not.

I cannot help speculating about Aunt Dorothy and Rossy. It is now over a week since I left Grosvenor Square.

I do wonder if they are awfully worried about me, and what they are doing.

I wonder if Harry is sorry that I've gone?

After all he did kiss me . . . once.

REFLECTION TWENTY-FOUR

Mr. Field kept coming in and out of the shop the whole of this morning.

I am afraid that Poppy is right, and that he is going to become rather tiresome, in which case I shall have to leave this job, I suppose.

It seems just like one of the stories I have read in the cheap magazines, when the heroine is invariably attacked by her employer.

What a nuisance it is sometimes being a girl, or at any rate an attractive one! Not that I am really grumbling, because it would be awful to be really plain.

I have sold a drawing-block, a packet of drawing-pins, and three pencils this morning. Really, trade has been quite brisk—I feel that is the right phrase.

Mr. Field had just been in for the umpteenth time.

He said, "Are you all right?" and I said, "Yes, perfectly," which was rather obvious, as I was sitting looking bright and, I hope, efficient behind the counter.

He said:

"Aren't you cold? Come down to the studio and get warm."

"No, thank you," I replied.

I said there was so much doing this morning that I had better be in the shop—it was less trouble than waiting downstairs for the bell to ring.

He sort of pottered about, and looked out of the window, and said:

"It's raining."

It is extraordinary how people talk about the weather when they can think of nothing to say, or are thinking about something quite different.

At last he went away, saying he must get back to work.

Then there has been another man behaving most peculiarly this morning. He is small and dark, rather cheaply dressed, but not poorly, and for a long time he looked in at the window, but he was not looking at the things which are spread in the window at all, but at me.

After a while he went away, and then came back and looked again.

I really felt quite embarrassed, so I turned my back and went to the darkest corner of the shop so that he could not see me. Then just now he came in and said:

"I want a paintbrush, please."

I got out the box they are kept in, but he did not take very much notice of them, felt one or two, and kept staring at me.

Then he said:

"Have you been here long?"

I did not know why, but it annoyed me, his inquisitiveness, so I said:

"Are these the sort of brushes you want?"

"No, no," he said, "I want a much bigger one."

"A bigger brush," I said, "or handle?"

He did not seem to know. He kept on staring, and then he said:

"Would you think it very rude of me if I asked your name?"

"Yes, very," I said. "If you do not want a paintbrush, I think you had better go away."

And with that he went, rather abashed, but when he got outside, he took something out of his pocket and looked at it.

Then he looked at me again through the glass—which luckily was so dark and dirty that it must have been very difficult for him to see much.

I wonder who he is, and why he is behaving like this. It seems to me very strange.

105

REFLECTION TWENTY-FIVE

Oh dear, such a lot of things have happened that my mind is quite chaotic.

First, I was sitting in the shop this afternoon when Mr. Field came in and said:

"Will you come downstairs? I've got something I want you to do."

He said it rather sharply, like an order, so of course I could not refuse to obey my employer. I went down into the studio, and he said:

"Will you please tidy these papers for me?"

He pointed to a small pile of bills, bits of string, labels and odd pencils, which were in a heap on the sofa—such a collection of rubbish, just as if one had upset a whole lot of things out of a drawer one had not used for some time.

However, I said yes, but he kept fidgeting about, and I could not help watching him to see why he was so restless.

Suddenly he said:

"What are you doing in this part of the world?"

"Trying to earn my living," I replied.

"Why did you leave your last job, if you had one?" he asked.

I replied, quite nicely, that it was for a private reason that I did not wish to discuss.

"Do you want to go back?" he said.

And I answered no, but that if I did I should go.

When I said this he walked up to where I was sitting trying to separate the papers into neat piles, and said:

"You'd better be very careful, then, because otherwise you may have to."

I was very surprised, and said:

"What do you mean . . . have to?"

"I know more about you than you think," he said.

The way he said it, in a sort of greasy, insinuating manner, annoyed me; and I replied, very coldly, that I did not see what my affairs had to do with him as long as I did my job competently and well.

"But I am very interested in you," he said, and sat down beside me on the sofa.

I got up at once, and said:

"I am afraid, Mr. Field, we are talking at cross-purposes. I think under the circumstances, it would be better if I went back to the shop, which is what I was engaged to look after."

"Not at all," he said. "You were engaged to do as I want, in the shop and studio."

I did not answer, but started to walk towards the door; but he got up quickly and, before I could stop him, got between me and the door.

"Now, now!" he said. "Don't be silly! I don't want to quarrel with you—that is the very last thing I want to do. But you don't want to be a silly little girl, do you, and have to go home again? After all, I ought to take you back. I know you are under age."

I was rather surprised at his saying all this, but at the same time I had a very strong feeling that he did not know half as much as he was pretending to, and that he was saying a lot of that to scare me and also to see what effect it would have on me.

"I have said before, Mr. Field," I remarked, "that I do not want to discuss my private affairs. May I please go?"

He laughed, and said:

"All right. I won't blackmail you, if you will pay me for keeping silent."

He put out his hands towards me, and I knew what sort of payment he required.

I stood there feeling quite desperate, and he made a step

107

towards me. I do not know what would have happened if at that moment the shop bell had not rung very hard.

Mr. Field stopped and looked disconcerted, and as quick as I could I slipped past him and opened the door and ran upstairs.

There, in the shop, was Uncle Lionel, and behind him was the funny little man who had tried to get into conversation with me in the morning.

I forgot everything, except how pleased I was to see Uncle Lionel. I flung my arms round his neck and kissed him, and he was awfully glad to see me too, and kept saying:

"Are you all right, Maxine? You are quite certain you are all right?" although I was looking particularly hale and hearty.

I seized my hat and coat and said:

"Come on . . . let's get away as soon as we can."

"Do you live here?" he asked, and I explained that I was only working there, and had just had a row with my employer.

"I do not want to see him again, and there is no need for explanations, anyway. Let's go!"

And though Uncle Lionel protested, I insisted on coming away, and we just walked out, without even saying good-bye to Mr. Field, so that ended my first job!

The odd little man who would stare at me was a detective, of course—I might have guessed that—and Uncle Lionel had had him looking everywhere to try and find me.

We went round to Poppy's tiny room, and Uncle Lionel nearly had a fit when he saw where I'd been living.

I must say after Grosvenor Square it was a bit of a change, but when we got in and the first excitement was wearing off I remembered why I had been obliged to run away.

Although I was pleased to see Uncle Lionel, because he had come at such an opportune moment, it was no use my going back to Grosvenor Square if I had to marry Rossy.

I asked Uncle Lionel about this, and he was most terribly nice. He said it was all a mistake, and Aunt Dorothy was frightfully upset—she hadn't really thought that I felt so strongly about it.

Of course I need not marry anybody I did not like; in fact he hoped I would not marry anyone for ages and ages, until I had had time to really make up my mind.

If I would come back now there would be no talk or suggestion of Rossy, and I need not even see him again if I did not want to.

He was really very kind, and very serious about it all. That made everything quite different and I said if that was the case I would come back.

Then I could not help asking if Aunt Dorothy was very angry with me for running away.

Uncle Lionel said she was very upset.

"And so was I, Maxine," he added. "You must never do such a thing again. We have been nearly off our heads with worry as to what had happened to you.

"Of course, I did not want to have it all in the papers, and I felt you would be sensible enough to let us know where you were, or come back to us. At the same time, I do not want to minimize the fact that you have caused us a great deal of pain and suffering."

After that, of course, I felt a perfect brute, and I told him how sorry I was, but it was just that I was desperate at the idea of being married off to Rossy, whom I hated.

Uncle Lionel said:

"If you had come to me, you know, I would not have allowed it. The whole thing was absurd and disgraceful."

He said this very sternly, and I could not help feeling that he must have said something of the sort when Aunt Dorothy told him why I had run away.

While we were talking, sitting on Poppy's bed, because there was only one chair in the room, Poppy came rushing in, and I introduced her to Uncle Lionel.

I must say he was very nice, and has the most charming manners, and I am sure Poppy liked him awfully.

Of course, he thanked her for looking after me, and I told him how kind she had been when I was ill.

"I am taking Maxine back with me now," Uncle Lionel said, "but I do hope you will come and see her often, and I know she will want to come and see you."

He said this quite simply, and Poppy was very pleased, and said of course she would, and that she would miss me frightfully.

I asked her if she thought Ivor was at home, because I must go over and explain to him.

"I think he'll be here in about five minutes," she replied, "if we wait."

So we all sat and waited and talked, and I never knew before that Uncle Lionel could be so amusing.

He made Poppy laugh like anything, and was really very witty about things—quite different from the way he is at Grosvenor Square with Aunt Dorothy's friends.

At the end he said to her:

"We must meet again, even apart from Maxine. I shall insist on your coming to dinner with me one night."

"I'd adore to," Poppy replied, "but nowhere too smart, remember!"

He laughed, and paid her some compliments which seemed to please her.

Just at that moment Ivor banged on the door and came in.

He was astounded to see Uncle Lionel, naturally, and somehow it was rather disappointing, but I don't think Uncle Lionel liked him much.

He stopped being gay and amusing, and became very severe and offhand, with what I call his 'politician' manner.

Ivor, who is very sensitive to other people's feelings, instantly became his very gruffest and most defiant, with that very 'I-am-not-afraid-to-fight' look which I noticed when I first met him, but which he quite drops when he is alone with me or with his own friends.

They talked very stiffly to each other, and Uncle Lionel thanked him too for having looked after me, but in a tone of voice as if he wished he had not.

I tried to make the peace by saying how nice Ivor had been, but this only seemed to make it worse, and we all got very stiff and formal.

I put my few things together in a parcel, and we went downstairs.

Outside, Uncle Lionel's Rolls was waiting.

The detective was sitting in front with the chauffeur, looking so smug and self-satisfied.

The landlady came out to say good-bye, awfully

impressed, and terribly gushing now she had seen Uncle Lionel's car.

But when it came to the point of leaving Poppy and Ivor I just could not bear it. I just could not help the tears coming into my eyes—they had both been so kind, and I loved staying with them.

I could not help feeling there was something fatal about my going away, as if things, or, rather, our friendship, could never be quite the same again.

I kissed Poppy, and I knew she was upset too, and then Ivor said:

"Good-bye—I'll telephone you some time," and walked off before I had time to answer.

So I knew he also felt my going because he would hate to show his emotion in an ordinary way.

I got into the car with Uncle Lionel, and waved and waved, but when we got to the corner and I looked back the only person waving was the old landlady, whom I had always disliked. Poppy and Ivor had disappeared.

When we got back to Grosvenor Square Aunt Dorothy greeted me most gushingly.

"What a silly girl you are," she said, "running away like that! But still, I have promised Lionel that I won't talk to you about it, so the whole subject is to be dropped . . . Oh, my dear, how you need a hair-wave, and your nails are shocking!"

I could not help laughing, because that was so typical of Aunt Dorothy. I am sure she thinks that is far more important than anything which has happened to me while I have been away. I said I would remedy that as soon as possible.

Now one funny thing has happened.

Since I have been away, though it is only such a short time really—years and years it seems!—I feel much more independent, and I am not frightened of Aunt Dorothy any more.

When I laughed at her then I realised that was something I'd never been able to do before, and that if I could go on and treat her and all her friends, and the whole situation as a joke, it would make things far easier, instead of my being so intense and worked up over everything.

Eleanor was tremendously glad to see me.

Mabel, Aunt Dorothy's maid, told me that Eleanor had wept her eyes out when I had gone, because she was so worried about me.

I do think it's rather sweet of her to be so fond of me, and I am glad somebody missed me as much as all that.

I never knew before how much I enjoyed a hot bath, and here I am lying in one and thinking about everything; and I must say it is rather nice to smell lovely bath-salts and to realise there is a really good dinner waiting for me.

I am afraid I must be a very superficial person to enjoy these things so much.

I wonder if I shall see Harry to-night, and what he thought when I was away, and whether I shall hear again from Rossy?

I hope Harry does not think that he had anything to do with my going—but of course he could not have, because I had explained it all to Aunt Dorothy, and I expect he saw the letter.

I do wish I knew if he has thought about me at all. I have thought a lot about him, in spite of trying not to.

I wonder if Ivor and Poppy are missing me now.

I must get up—but I do like this hot bath!

REFLECTION TWENTY-SIX

Things have changed absolutely.

It is all most peculiar! I am being treated now exactly like a *débutante*.

Apparently Uncle Lionel had a long talk with Aunt Dorothy, and from what I gather there was a tremendous row between them when I left.

No one has exactly told me about it, but everyone has dropped hints, said a little and then stopped.

I have patched the whole thing together, until I know, more or less accurately, what happened.

Uncle Lionel blamed Aunt Dorothy entirely, and said that as she had promised to bring me out she had got to do so properly. He would not have me going about with any odd person who happened to ask me, or going to night clubs.

I was to attend proper *débutante* dances, and for the rest of the season do all the things which *débutantes* are supposed to do.

Aunt Dorothy of course was very reluctant, but as he was so angry she had to agree and do what he wanted.

He so seldom puts his foot down that when he does apparently everyone, even Aunt Dorothy, obeys him.

Anyhow, she has in this case, and I am being taken

nightly to real balls, properly chaperoned—complete with white kid gloves and a programme!

It is all really very funny, and it makes me laugh.

The sad thing is that I really find them rather boring now—by 'them' I mean the balls, the other *débutantes*, the chaperonage, and the young men.

If I had done this the moment I arrived in London I should have enjoyed it very much.

But now, having spent a month going about with Aunt Dorothy's crowd, and with Ivor and Poppy, I cannot sort of put myself back.

I must say she does her part extremely well, now that she has made up her mind to it, and I am not certain that sometimes she does not enjoy herself.

If there is a nice man, or a nice 'young-old' man at the dances, they are so thrilled to see a really smart, good-looking woman amongst all the giggling girls that Aunt Dorothy has a tremendous success.

I have come to the conclusion that girls *en masse* are terrible. If I were a man, I should marry a widow of over thirty-five.

I have seen Harry once since I have been back. He looked at me in a funny speculative sort of way and said:

"If you were in trouble why didn't you ask me to help you?"

I was so surprised that I could not think of an answer and he went on:

"I will always help you, Maxine, you know that."

"You didn't . . . say . . . so," I stammered.

"I thought you understood," he said crossly, "we've all been off our heads wondering what had happened to you."

"I thought . . . perhaps you would be . . . glad to be . . . rid of me," I faltered.

"How can you be so stupid?" he asked quite angrily.

I was so surprised that I could not think of an answer. Then Aunt Dorothy called me and I had to leave him.

There is more excitement!

Apparently he and Aunt Dorothy have practically separated or whatever is done when a love affair is over—and it really is over.

Or so I gather from something Baba said, but Aunt

Dorothy is very upset about it, I believe, because I think she really loves him.

Anyway, Harry has sort of drifted away, and when I do see him he is quite nice to me, but rather offhand to Aunt Dorothy.

She keeps trying to be awfully nice, and it is rather pathetic. He came at tea-time, and she said things like:

"I got this *paté* you like so much specially for you, Harry"; and, "I ordered these biscuits because I know you like them."

It seemed to me as if she were trying to please him, like a mother with a tiresome child who won't eat.

After all they had meant to each other, if she has had to come down to trying to entice him through his food, it really seems rather terrible, and also very sad.

Poor Aunt Dorothy!

The awful thing is that I believe the whole thing is my fault, because apparently when Uncle Lionel was so angry about my running away he added in a row about Harry as well, and said he would not have it.

Of course, Poppy is quite right—Aunt Dorothy does not love Harry enough to run away with him and give up this lovely house and her position in Society.

So I suppose she has had to make the best of a bad job and do what Uncle Lionel wants.

I am going to another dance to-night, which promises to be brighter than the other ones I have been to lately.

It is what they call a 'young married' dance, and is to be given at the most lovely house in Park Lane, which belongs to the smartest and most talked-of 'young married' in London, who is very nearly Royalty she is so important.

Aunt Dorothy has got me a new dress for it, and we are going, a party of twelve, dining here first.

I don't know, but I have a feeling as if something quite exciting might happen to me to-night, and I do hope it does, because I don't know why, not even to myself, but I have been a little bored lately.

That sounds awful, as though one was only amused when people were making love to one, but really, after all the excitement of the first weeks I was in London, to settle down to the bread-and-butter of *débutantes'* balls has been a little bit dull.

115

No one has even so much as paid me a compliment, except the old fathers of the *débutantes*, and among all the thousands of awful youths I have danced with the nicest thing said to me was:

"I say, you do dance rippingly!"

I cannot be expected to get much of a thrill out of that, after having been made love to by Timmy and Ivor, and of course . . . Harry.

REFLECTION TWENTY-SEVEN

I was quite right—last night was thrilling.

To begin with, the house was lovely, and the people were all very amusing and most interesting to see.

They were much more the Embassy type that I saw so much of before I was made back into a *débutante*.

The women were all incredibly thin, with wonderful dresses, which fitted so tightly that they looked as though they had been poured into them, and their jewels were marvellous.

They moved about in a sort of willowy fashion, and said "Darling, this is too divine!" whenever they met an acquaintance.

It was all very gay and unusual—the atmosphere I mean—while at a *débutante* party the air seems sort of heavy, like pudding—though that's a *cliché* I know I ought not to use.

Ivor would be furious! But there is that sort of sodden, heavy feeling, rather like a damp cake, while at last night's party the air was crisp and frosty—not really, of course, but that is how it felt.

Everyone seemed determined to sparkle, and be brighter, and gayer, and more amusing than anyone else. It was as though everyone was on tiptoe, on the very top of their form.

The fact that the Prince of Wales was there may have had something to do with it, but he was treated quite ordinarily, as if he were just 'Mr. Wales'.

No one made a stupid fuss, or stared, or anything like that, and he seemed to be enjoying himself frightfully.

I did hope—I could not help it!—that perhaps by some wonderful chance, he might want to dance with me.

But he did not have very many partners, just two or three women he knew, and, of course, our hostess, who looked perfectly lovely, and I did envy her!

However, Aunt Dorothy introduced me to one or two men, so I had plenty of partners, including of course, the men we had brought with us in our party.

Then I ran into Mona, looking very smart, and far older and more sophisticated than most of the married women there.

She said, "Maxine, darling"—talking in that same rather affected way that they all do—"I do want to introduce Alec Beattoc. He's too divine—I know you will adore each other!"

I shook hands with a tall, very good-looking young man with fair hair and quite the bluest eyes I've ever seen.

He was really incredibly good-looking, and danced better than anyone I've ever danced with before, and he is most frightfully amusing, and made me laugh so much.

It was not only what he said—which, as it happened, was very witty and intelligent—but also the way he said it.

He is very popular, and everybody talked to us as we danced round, and he had a word or a joke to share with everybody.

He also talked in that same "darling" and "divine" manner, but he did it quite naturally, and somehow I did not object to it, like I should have thought I would have.

We danced and danced, and then we sat out and talked and talked, and I cannot possibly remember all he said, but I know there seemed an endless fund of things to discuss.

Yet none of it was very serious, only he seemed to make me feel as though I was being very witty and clever too—which is a lovely feeling!

I asked him to tell me all about himself, and apparently he is an "Honourable", and his father is Lord Something-

or-other—I have forgotten the name—and he is very poor, and has tried all sorts of jobs to make money.

He has even tried journalism, where he has been a great success, because he is so humorous, and he is so popular that luckily he never wants for invitations to meals or parties.

His father lives in Ireland, and, according to Alec, they have an old castle in the middle of a bog, which is falling to rack and ruin for want of repairs.

All the money they have goes on horses, so that the whole family—apparently there are lots of them—can hunt.

The way he told the story made it very romantic and exciting, and then he said:

"Now tell me about yourself. You are Mayfair's latest little heiress, aren't you? What fun—because you do not need to be one, with your looks!"

I said I believed one day I should have some money, but I did not know when, or what.

He laughed and said:

"That's right. Never worry about money—unless you have not got it—and then forget it!"

That does not sound a bit funny when I think about it now, but it is the way Alec says things, and he has a queer trick or raising one eyebrow which is most attractive, at least I think so.

I do not know how long we should have gone on talking if a perfectly lovely creature had not come up and said:

"I am furious with you, Alec! You have cut my dance."

"Darling," he said, "I'm devastated—do forgive me. I am really an awful person—I often have to cut myself for weeks!"—or some such nonsense.

Of course the 'lovely creature' could not help laughing and forgiving him.

"Very well, come and finish this encore with me," Alec said and added to me:

"I will ring you up to-morrow, Maxine. Don't forget."

I was terribly complimented to think he had cut a dance with such a 'lovely creature' so as to talk to me.

As it was very late, I came home then with Aunt Dorothy, who had enjoyed herself very much and got off with all sorts of young men.

She really did look smart. Her dress was of deep blue

sequins, and she wore a sapphire and diamond necklace and absolutely masses of bracelets.

We came home in the car, both very sleepy, but quite 'purry' with enjoyment to think what fun it had been. As I fell into bed the last thing I thought of was Alec, and I was awakened by the telephone pealing in my ear.

It was eleven o'clock, and it was Alec wanting to speak to me.

"Good morning, red-headed siren!" he said. "How late you are! I've been awake quite ten minutes."

Of course that woke me up, to think that he had wanted to ring me up the moment he was awake, and I said:

"Wasn't last night fun?"

"A divine thing happened to me," he said.

"What?" I asked.

"Meeting you," he replied. "You are an awful creature too. Do you know I have dreamed about you all night?"

"How thrilling!" I said. "What did you dream?"

"Tut-tut!" he said. "I thought you were supposed to be a *débutante*!"

We went on talking all sorts of rubbish for ages and ages, and then he asked if he could come to lunch.

I said of course, I was sure he could, and if by any chance Aunt Dorothy had arranged anything else I would ring him up, but I was sure it would be all right.

He rang off, and I sent Eleanor down to ask Aunt Dorothy; and now a message has just come back to say it is quite all right.

I really am frightfully excited, and it will be fun to see him again.

I do hope he will be as nice this morning as he was last night.

I cannot make up my mind if I shall look my best in my green dress, which I have not worn yet, or the white *crêpe-de-Chine* with the black belt.

What a problem clothes are! Men are lucky not to have to worry so much. I wonder which he would like me best in? I think perhaps the green—I know green goes well with my hair.

Ivor has just rung up, but I really have not got time to see him to-day.

At least I suppose I have this afternoon, but I don't know—I might be asked to do something else.

Perhaps Aunt Dorothy will want me to do something with her. Anyway, I have refused him now, so it does not matter.

... Yes, I think definitely I will wear the green!

REFLECTION TWENTY-EIGHT

I have just been for a walk in the Park with Alec. It is the most lovely day I have ever seen.

I have never seen the Park look nicer. The flowers are absolutely gorgeous, and how happy and gay everyone looked!

I do like Alec.

He really is charming, and he does seem to think everything one says is interesting—so unlike a lot of men who are so busy talking themselves they never listen to what you say.

Of course, he is absurdly good-looking. People are always talking about 'like a Greek god'.

I have never seen a Greek god—at least I do not think so; I mean of course, a statue or a reproduction of one—but I imagine that, if they are very good-looking, that is what Alec looks like.

We walked quite a long way, right down to the Serpentine, and he insisted on pushing that fat, spoilt Lulu into the water.

Lulu was furious, but it really was very funny, and I have had to smuggle him upstairs for Mabel to dry before Aunt Dorothy sees him, or she would be frightfully angry. She simply dotes on that dog.

Personally, if I had a dog of my own, I would never

have a Pekinese. I would have something much bigger and more sporting-looking.

It was great fun and we talked all sorts of nonsense, and sat about on the chairs until we saw the ticket-collector coming, when Alec sprang to his feet and said:

"Come on! We cannot afford fourpence."

And I said I had it, and he said:

"Nonsense! I'm Irish. I always run away and never pay. Irishmen can always run faster than anyone else, so they never get caught!"

It seems rather silly now, but at the time it was a great joke, and we ran away right up the hill, to where 'Rima' stands in that funny little garden.

Alec was quite preposterous, and pranced up to a very pompous-looking man who was looking at the sculpture, and said:

"Excuse me sir, but can you tell me if this is consecrated ground?"

"Certainly not, sir!" replied the man.

I think he realised that Alec was not serious, because I was laughing so much.

We went round to where all the Nannies sit with the babies, and Alec would peer into all the perambulators and say:

"What a charming baby! Exactly like my ninth grandchild."

And the Nannies did not know whether to be angry or amused, except one, who said:

"Sh! She's asleep!"

Alec then tiptoed away in an exaggerated fashion, and all the others simply had to laugh. Altogether quite a mad afternoon, but such fun.

When we got back I found Uncle Lionel had just come from the House, and he said:

"Maxine, I want to speak to you for a moment."

"I'll go into the drawing-room," Alec said, "I expect your aunt is there."

So I went into Uncle Lionel's room, and he said:

"I have been thinking things over, Maxine, and I think it would be a good thing if you had your own banking account.

"You are quite old enough to realise the proper value of

money. I have just been talking to Miss Roberts, and she is very upset because you spent so much in the last month."

"How awful," I said. "Have I spent all I have got?"

He smiled and said:

"Not quite all. Have you any idea how much you have got?"

None, I said, except that Mummy had told me that one day I should have a little money of my own.

"I think you ought to know," he said, "that one day—in fact, a day not very far off, when you are twenty-one—you come into a very large amount of money left to you by your father.

"When your mother dies, you will of course have still more, which naturally we hope will not be for a great many years.

"But in two years' time you will be, to all intents and purposes, a very rich girl, and I want you to start now re-alising the responsibilities that money brings, and that it is not all fun having a large income.

"You are responsible not only to yourself and your trustees, of which, as you know, I am one, but also to the community for the handling of your money.

"I do not want to sound pompous, or to preach to you in any way, but I do think that at such a time in history money can be used, as never before, not only for good, but definitely harmfully.

"Therefore, Maxine, I want you to think a good deal in the ensuing two years of how you are going to behave when this money is entrusted to you.

"Within bounds, you will be a quite free agent, to do as you like with it, and I do want you to think about this and have some definite ideas on the subject.

"Should you marry in the meantime, the money be-comes yours at once, and so I hope you will choose a man who will help you spend wisely and well.

"While we are talking of marriage, I do not want to up-set you in any way, but I think you ought to realise that there are men in the world who would be very pleased just now to marry a girl with money of her own, especially a girl as attractive as you are.

"I want you to choose your friends very carefully and

because you are certain they are sincere in their affection for you."

I said yes, very solemnly, and that I would be very careful and think over all Uncle Lionel had told me, and I said:

"Tell me, Uncle Lionel, how much shall I have? I would like to know."

"Unless the Government does something still more peculiar with the income tax," he said, "you will have about twelve thousand pounds a year when you are twenty-one. But for the next two years I intend to allow you four thousand pounds a year to dress on and amuse yourself."

Of course it seems to me millions and millions, and I am absolutely astounded. I had no idea that I should be so rich.

It is awfully thrilling, and I am quite excited about it; yet at the same time just a little frightened, in case, as Uncle Lionel said, I do a lot of harm.

I went up to the drawing-room in a very subdued mood, but Alec soon made me laugh again.

One or two people had come in, and they also were very amused by Alec, and I think Aunt Dorothy likes him.

She has known him, vaguely, for years, but he has not actually been to the house before.

I am very glad she likes him, because I think she will ask him again, and I do want to see lots and lots of Alec, because he is such a very nice person.

REFLECTION TWENTY-NINE

I do not know what is the matter with me. I am all dissatisfied and cross.

It is silly, I know, because I ought to be so happy. The weather's lovely. I have been to such amusing parties, and I am looking forward to Ascot.

Aunt Dorothy has bought me the most wonderful clothes, but I just feel upset, as though I wanted something—I am not quite certain what I do want.

It is awfully silly to be like this, and I am really very angry with myself.

Perhaps I am over-tired, and yet I feel very well, and even if I am up late I sleep nearly till lunch-time, so there is no excuse for getting like this.

I wish I knew what Alec really thought about me. He is terribly sweet, and awfully complimentary, but that is not quite what I mean.

I never seem to get any closer—no, that is the wrong word—sort of get to know him better.

We talk and laugh, and chatter just the same as we did the first night. He rushes into the house and says:

"Darling, it is too thrilling to see you!"

Then he starts to tell me something quite fantastic which has happened, and I think what fun it all is, and how much I love having him for a friend.

But that is all there is to it, and I suppose I must be truthful and confess to myself that I want more—that I want Alec to be in love with me, and to make love to me.

Somehow he does not seem to want to do that.

There have been masses of opportunities—we have been driven together in cars, sat together on balconies at dances, or even in a garden in the moonlight.

Although he always calls me 'darling' and holds my hand, he has never tried to kiss me, or said 'darling' in the real meaning way.

After all, words only mean what one intends them to express, and 'darling' said by Alec does not mean really anything.

Everyone in the older crowd seems to call each other 'darling' the whole time, and I think it is only a sort of catch-phrase, like many of their other expressions.

I don't know . . . I wish I did not feel like this about the whole thing, but last night we went to Mona's house, and Aunt Dorothy did not have to come, because Mona's mother was sufficient chaperon.

I think she was very glad, by the way, because she had a date with a young man at the Embassy.

So I went off alone in the car, and when I got there I knew everybody, including, of course, Alec, whom Mona had asked, very tactfully, I thought.

We sat together at dinner, and afterwards there was a sort of impromptu dance to the electric gramophone, which was the greatest fun.

There were about twenty-five couples, and no formal supper, or anything like that, only some sandwiches and eggs-and-bacon.

At about three o'clock I thought I had better go home, having enjoyed myself awfully.

The car was waiting for me, and Alec said:

"I will come with you, Maxine. Can the car drop me afterwards? I do not live very far away."

Of course I said that was all right, and we started off just alone together in Uncle Lionel's big Rolls.

It was a very silent and black night, and the streets were quite deserted, and I felt all sort of warm and happy, with a big rug cuddled over my knees.

Alec took my hand, slipping his arm through mine, and I moved as close to him as I could.

"Tired, darling?" he asked.

"Just a little bit," I replied, "but so happy."

He squeezed my hand, and I looked at him sideways, but he was not looking at me, but straight in front of him, with his profile against the window.

He really looked too marvellously good-looking to be true, and I could not help—though I hate myself for it now—just moving my head the tiniest bit, so that it rested against his shoulder.

He could easily have bent his head and kissed me. It was the easiest thing possible, but somehow he did not do it.

After a minute I felt cold and disappointed, and something which had felt warm and confiding in me felt very snubbed, and of course I could not say anything.

Before I could really even think, we had arrived, and we got out, and he said:

"Good night, and sleep well, beautiful one. I will ring you up in the morning."

I went up to bed feeling all sorts of strange things, wondering and upset. I cannot think why he did not kiss me, because he must have known that I wanted him to.

REFLECTION THIRTY

I am furious with Harry. I cannot think why I ever
thought he was nice. I think he is interfering, extremely
impertinent, and a beast.

It all happened yesterday.

I had had the most charming luncheon at the Ritz with
Mona, who I really do like very much, and who is so
beautiful if only she did not try to dress like her own
mother.

Alec was there, and a friend of Mona's, a very nice
man in the Navy. Alec was perfectly charming to me, and
I was so happy, and enjoying myself tremendously.

After luncheon we talked outside for a bit, and then
Mona and her boy friend went off to go to a cinema.

Alec and I sat in the kind of palm court at the top of
the steps in the corner, where there are two enormous
armchairs, very close together, and where one can almost
hide from the people walking up and down the passage-
way.

We talked and talked about ourselves and all sorts of
things, and Alec was very serious for once, and told me
that he was rather depressed over financial difficulties.

His father had said that if he could not get a job he
would have to give up his flat—which is only a tiny

one—and go back to live in Ireland, where at least the rent was free.

"Oh, Alec, I am so sorry," I said. "Don't go back to Ireland!"

"Do you really mean that, Maxine?" he said and caught hold of my hand.

He was just going to say something—and I cannot help thinking it was something I wanted terribly to hear—when there was a step beside us, and there was Harry.

Alec said, "Hullo, Harry!" not very cordially, I thought, and I echoed, "Hullo!" And Alec dropped my hand.

Or I think I took it away, feeling rather silly, because it was obvious we were saying something very confidential.

Our faces were very close to each other, and we did not know quite how long Harry had been watching us. There wasn't anyone on the sofas near us, so we had thought ourselves quite alone.

Harry said:

"Your aunt wants you, Maxine, and has asked me to take you back to Grosvenor Square. I have a car outside."

So, of course, I had to say good-bye to Alec.

Anyway, it was not for very long, for he was coming to dinner to-night.

I walked outside and got into the car. I must say it is a very nice one of Harry's, a Bentley, but his chauffeur was driving, so we sat behind.

"Look here, Maxine," he said, "your aunt does not really want you, but I had something I wanted to say to you."

"Aunt Dorothy does not really want me?" I echoed. "What do you mean? Why did you say she did?"

"I have been watching you for some time with young Beattoc," he said, "and before you get too involved with that young man I think you ought to know something about him."

I asked what he meant by 'involved', and said I did know lots about Alec, anyway.

Harry looked very grave, and he talked rather slowly and seriously, and even though I was so surprised and beginning to get rather angry, I could not help thinking that he was very attractive.

But I did not think that for long, because he began to annoy me so much.

"I don't think young Beattoc is a good companion for you," he said. "I don't think Dolly realises the truth about him, but anyway you had better ask her what she thinks."

I said Aunt Dorothy liked Alec very much, and anyway, I hated hearing insinuations about my friends, and if he had anything against Alec I should like to hear it straight out.

Harry hummed and ha'd, and then he said that Alec was a well-known young waster, and was in a bad financial way.

But he said this as though it was not the most important thing, and I knew there was something else as well.

And I said I was quite aware that Alec had no money, but I still did not see what that had to do with our friendship or with him—Harry—interfering.

"Damn it all, Maxine," Harry said, "it is frightfully difficult to explain to you, but he is no good, you know— take it from me. I'm years older than both of you, and Alec Beattoc is no use to you as a young man, but he is heavily in debt, and he may take it into his head to get married."

"Why shouldn't he get married if he wants to?" I asked.

"Not to you, anyway," Harry said.

Then I got really angry, and said I should marry whom I liked, and that I was quite sure that Alec could do without any interference from outsiders.

"I tell you he's a little rotter," said Harry. "I can't put it stronger!"

"I did not know that you were such a Sir Galahad yourself," I said as nastily as I could.

Harry was perfectly furious, and said:

"You are an obstinate little fool, Maxine, but I don't blame you. It is this blasted innocence which is so difficult to compete with."

I said it was all very well to abuse me for being innocent, but he would not actually say what he thought was wrong with Alec, except that he was running after me for my money.

I was the best judge of whether anyone was in love with me for my money or not!

131

"Oh, it is not that," Harry said. "It is no use talking to you—I shall speak to your uncle."

Then I began to get rather frightened because I did not want Uncle Lionel dragged into another trouble over me, but anyway it was nothing to do with Harry who I went out with, as Aunt Dorothy approved.

I said all this, and also told Harry that I did not see what there was to tell Uncle Lionel, because I was not even engaged to Alec, and—if Harry must know—he had not even proposed to me.

"But he is going to," said Harry. "I can see it all blowing up to that, and I won't have it—do you hear, Maxine?"

By this time we had arrived at Grosvenor Square and I stalked indoors, followed by Harry.

Nobody seemed to be at home, so we went into the drawing-room and went on talking in the same strain, and Harry would not say exactly what he had against Alec.

At last I got perfectly mad, and I said:

"I shall ring Alec and ask him to come here, and you can tell him to his face, in front of me, what you have against him."

"Do as you like," Harry said, "but I am also going to speak to your uncle—that is what you are afraid of, isn't it?"

He was so frightfully irritating, and we had argued and been so rude to each other, that I just stamped my foot and shouted:

"I shall do as I like! Go away—and please mind your own business!"

I was so angry that tears came into my eyes.

Harry started to reply, when suddenly the door opened and in walked Uncle Lionel.

"What is going on here?" he said.

I was so upset that I could not even explain, but just slipped past him upstairs to my room, and I could not help crying a little from pure rage.

Then I rang up Alec on the telephone, and said to him:

"I hate Harry! He's beastly to me!"

Alec asked what was the matter, and then of course I realised that I could not tell him exactly what it was, and he said:

132

"Darling, don't let anybody upset you—it's too revolting. Shall I come round and cheer you up?"

I said I thought he had better wait till dinner-time, as we were meeting then anyway.

"I've got such a lot to say to you, Maxine," he said.

There was a pause and then he added, in a very quiet voice:

"I suppose you know what I want to say?"

I said no rather doubtfully, and he said:

"Is it 'yes' or 'no', Maxine?"

Then he laughed, and added:

"I think it will be rather fun getting married, don't you?"

"Do you mean that, Alec?" I said.

"Of course," he replied.

"Well—it's 'yes'."

And I thought to myself:

"That's done Harry, anyhow!"

Alec said:

"Lovely, lovely! What fun! I'll talk to you about it to-night, but don't let's tell anybody just yet."

"Of course not," I said.

Then after a moment or two we rang off, and I could not help thinking how funny it was to be proposed to on the telephone; but I felt awfully modern, and very twentieth-centuryish.

I was so excited. I jumped about my room, thinking how lovely it all was.

But in about two minutes there was a knock at the door, and Eleanor brought me a message from Uncle Lionel to say would I go down and see him.

Somehow I had a premonition that something nasty was going to happen, and I thought, "Oh, I don't want to go", but of course I had to, and I went down to the library.

Uncle Lionel was alone, so I supposed that Harry had gone.

"I expect, Maxine," he said, "you know why I have sent for you."

"I suppose because Harry has been telling you a number of lies," I said.

"Well, I should like to think they were lies," said Uncle

Lionel, "but I don't think Harry has anything to gain by inventing stories against your friend."

"What has he said?" I asked very defiantly. "That Alec was trying to marry me for my money, and what else?"

Uncle Lionel seemed rather embarrassed, and he took up a paper-knife and played about with it.

"You are not a child, Maxine," he said, "but there are one or two things in the world which there is no point in your knowing about.

"Certain things which—how shall I put it?—offend against decency, but which are often ignored because people don't wish to make a scandal."

"I do not know what all this is about," I said. "I do not understand. What has this got to do with Alec? How could he offend against decency when everybody likes him and he knows everybody?"

Uncle Lionel took my hand and said:

"Look here, Maxine—you know I am terribly fond of you. You know I would do anything in my power to help you out of any trouble, or to give you anything you particularly wanted. But on this occasion I ask you to trust my judgment, without explanation.

"And though Harry Standish has told me things against your friend, I will do everything in my power to find out the truth of what he says, and if possible prove it untrue.

"But until I have done so will you give me your word of honour that you will not become engaged to him."

"I am engaged to him, Uncle Lionel."

"In that case I must see the young man myself," he said.

"Do tell me," I begged. "Do explain."

"I cannot do that, Maxine," Uncle Lionel replied. "Anyway, as things have gone so far, I think it is only fair for me to speak to the boy myself. I will do this before I say anything more to you about the matter. Will you give me his telephone number?"

So I gave him Alec's telephone number, and Uncle Lionel sent for him there and then, and here I am sitting in my room utterly miserable and wondering what is going on downstairs.

Oh dear! Oh dear! Just a little while ago I was so terribly happy, and everything had seemed as if it had come all right, but now Harry has spoilt everything, and I hate him—I do, really.

I hate him and if I get the chance to be as unkind to him as he has been to me I shan't hesitate to take it!

REFLECTION THIRTY-ONE

I do not understand what has happened. All I know is that if this is grown-up life I wish to goodness I was back at the convent again.

There at least one did know what would happen from hour to hour and day to day, and if it was monotonous, it was at any rate sane monotony.

Here I seem to be living in a mad world, where things and situations bob up at a moment's notice and disappear just as quickly.

I do not know what happened between Alec and Uncle Lionel, and, as far as I can make out, I never shall know.

Uncle Lionel sent for me just before dinner.

I had been sitting in my bedroom for what seemed to me hours and hours, and it had got darker and darker and I had not bothered to put on the light.

Then Eleanor came and fetched me, and I went downstairs. Uncle Lionel was frightfully serious and rather depressed. He said:

"I feel sure you will be very angry with me, Maxine, and perhaps very disappointed, when I tell you that I am afraid your friendship with Alec Beattoc has finished."

"Has it really finished?" I said. "But why should it? I want to see Alec and talk to him myself."

"I am afraid you cannot do that, Maxine," Uncle Lionel replied. "I have had a talk with the young man and . . ."

There he hesitated, and then went on:

"I think there is no need to go into any explanations. He asked me to tell you how sorry he was, but circumstances have forced him to leave London for the time being, and he has gone to his father's home in Ireland."

"Circumstances, I suppose, being you and Harry," I said. "What is it, and why is it? You must be blackmailing him, or something."

Uncle Lionel looked very severe and said:

"There is some blackmail which I consider entirely legitimate. I am sorry to tell you, Maxine, this young man who is outwardly very charming, is utterly worthless to you.

"If I had not known his father all my life I should feel obliged to take severer measures than those I have already taken and intend to take. As it is, I can only commiserate with my old friend for having produced such a son."

"But what has he done?" I asked again.

"Surely it is enough for you to know that he is a decadent product of a decadent age," Uncle Lionel said. "And that while you are under my care and my roof I do not intend to see you sacrificed or spoilt by association with such people."

Then he stopped being severe, and tried to be very nice and said:

"Cheer up, Maxine—you are very young. You will find that you will forget quite easily. After all, this flirtation has not gone very far, has it?"

Of course I could not say it had, as Alec had never even kissed me, but I do wonder what he has done, and why Uncle Lionel was so severe about it.

He just refused to talk about it any more after that, and I knew it was no use asking him, but I cannot help wondering and wondering.

What is the most awful thing that anyone can do?

If he had cheated at cards, or forged a cheque, or anything like that, surely Uncle Lionel would not have talked about decadence. But still, I suppose it is no use worrying.

I shall never know until I see Alec again, and then I shall ask him outright, but it must have been something very dreadful, or Alec would never have left London in the middle of the season.

I know he adores all the parties and loathes being stuck in some out-of-the-way place where he cannot dance or have a gay time with lots of friends.

He has told me that so often and yet at one word from Uncle Lionel he leaves for Ireland!

I do not understand it—I do not, really—and I think I am dreadfully unhappy. I shall miss him so much, I know I shall, but of course the whole thing is Harry's fault.

If he had not told Uncle Lionel no one would have made all this fuss, and even if I had not married Alec I could have gone on being friends with him for ever and ever.

Oh, how Harry annoys me!

If I had not been so awfully worried I could have turned round and told Uncle Lionel himself about Harry.

But of course I would not let down Aunt Dorothy, and I really could not do such a thing, because I think that is a cad's trick. But still Harry deserves it.

He must have trusted me very much, or he might have been frightened that I should have told Uncle Lionel about him.

I wonder why he minded so much, or why it mattered to him who I was friends with.

It seems odd that he should worry, or take the trouble to make a fuss!

I am quite exhausted, and tired of the whole thing. The funny part is that I have not cried a single tear since Uncle Lionel said I was not to see Alec any more.

I should have thought I'd cry and cry, but I have not. I wonder why not? That seems silly, wondering why one does not cry, but still it is unlike me.

REFLECTION THIRTY-TWO

I have met Rossy again, and I really feel I was rather unkind to him. He came up most humbly to speak to me at Ascot.

Oh, how lovely Ascot was—I did enjoy myself! My dresses were quite a riot, and I was photographed and put in all the papers as 'a beautiful *débutante*'.

I am so excited about it!

I cut all the pictures out and sent them to Mummy, and I do hope she will be pleased.

I think if you have children it must be very gratifying when they are a public success, and I do feel I was a success at Ascot, because everyone congratulated me on my get-ups.

We only went on two days, because Aunt Dorothy says it is not done to go on four. Personally, I should have adored to go, but she said no, so we went Wednesday and Thursday.

I wore green on the Wednesday, and the most lovely white chiffon on Cup Day.

I have never been so thrilled by anything as the Royal procession. It was just like a fairy story, with all the crowds and the green course.

I wish I could think about it properly all over again. I am so bad at expressing myself too, and I did try and write it all down in my letter to Mummy, although of course she knows it herself already.

But I do think writing down helps one to remember things, and I want to remember my first Ascot as long as I live.

I cannot understand how people can be *blasé* about it. Two or three young married women said to me:

"I cannot think why you want to go. I loathe Ascot—just a glorified garden party, with a smell of horseflesh in the distance!"

I may be very unsmart, but I enjoyed every minute, and I simply longed to go again on Friday, but Aunt Dorothy would not let me.

Anyway, I saw Rossy on Wednesday, among thousands of other people, and he said:

"Don't be angry with me, Maxine—do please let me come and see you some time."

I promised that he should, and I dare say he is much nicer than I thought. I feel so much older and wiser now, and perhaps it was very silly and over-excited of me to run away as I did.

REFLECTION THIRTY-THREE

Ivor is terribly ill. I have just come from Chelsea, and I am so upset, and can hardly think.

I got the message about two hours ago from Poppy.

I had been out the whole day, and she had rung up three or four times, and when I got back I'd only been in two minutes before she rang again.

"Maxine, Ivor has got double pneumonia," she said. "Can you come and see him? He has been asking for you."

"Oh, Poppy, how dreadful!" I said. "Of course I will come at once."

I rushed downstairs and stopped the car just as it was going back to the garage. I left a message to tell Uncle Lionel where I'd gone, and told the chauffeur to drive like hell.

Poppy met me on the doorstep. She said Ivor was taken ill two days ago, and of course he would not have the doctor till last night, when he was so bad and so queer that she was terrified.

The doctor says that he ought to go to a nursing-home, but Ivor has made such a fuss that they do not dare move him at the moment because he is so bad that being upset might hurt him.

"We don't know what to do, or how to make him do as

he's told," Poppy said. "There is a nurse here, and she and I are taking turns to nurse him. She is lying down at the moment, because she has got to be up all night."

I went to Ivor's room, and there he was, looking too dreadful, so pale and ill.

He is always thin, but it seemed as if being ill had made him look absolutely wasted.

In spite of being upset I could not help thinking how he himself had always said that modern women, because they were so thin, looked like starving Russia—that is just what he looked like himself.

I was not really being frivolous, because I was very near to tears.

It was just one of those thoughts which keep pushing into one's head—usually, I think, when one is upset, one thinks of irrelevant things.

I sat down beside him. He was breathing in an awfully funny way. I touched his hand, and he opened his eyes and tried to smile at me, but it was obviously a fearful effort.

"Hurry up and get well, Ivor," I said. "This is naughty of you."

He smiled again, and I said:

"Will you go to a nursing-home? . . . Please!"

He shook his head, and tried to speak. We could not hear what he said, except something about the 'rich' and I said:

"Oh, do not be silly, Ivor—it is far more important to get well."

But he still shook his head, and I saw it was beginning to worry him, so I did not say any more, but just sat quietly and held his hand.

The light was very dim in the room, and it all seemed very quiet and peaceful and after a little while I think he dropped asleep. Poppy beckoned me, and I just tiptoed from the room, and she said: "I'm sure you've done him good. He seems more peaceful—he was so restless all last night and all to-day."

"He isn't really dying?" I said.

"No," she said, "but he's very bad and he's so pig-headed the doctor almost despairs of making him do what

142

he wants. But the nurse is awfully nice, and she was looking after him the whole night."

I gave Poppy five pounds, and said:

"You've simply got to take it, for Ivor, and don't you dare tell him that I've given it, because you know how funny he is about money. But get anything he wants, and please send the doctor's bill to me."

"You're a brick, Maxine," Poppy said. "I don't suppose he will let me do that, but I'll buy anything he wants with this."

She kissed me good-bye, but she looked rather peaky and queer, and I cannot help thinking that Poppy is a little bit in love with Ivor, in spite of all the things she says about the man she lived with.

Ivor likes her very much, but I do not think in that way, because he told me once he did not admire her type at all.

I do hope she is not in love with him, and that I am just imagining things, but it does seem as though she was frightfully devoted to him, and only too eager to do anything she can for him.

I do hope Ivor gets well. I am really so very worried. However, I am more hopeful since I have come back and have just told Uncle Lionel about it. He was very sweet though I still think he does not like Ivor much.

He rang the doctor up—luckily I remembered his name, because he was the one who came to me when I had that chill—and told him, if he was at all anxious, to call in a specialist and send the bill to him, Uncle Lionel.

I was very grateful to him, because it took a big load off my mind.

After all, Ivor was very sweet to me and very kind, and all the time I was in Chelsea he tried to look after me and do everything he could for me, and there was no reason why he should at all.

I feel sure he will get better. It would be awful if he died.

Not that I think Ivor is afraid of dying. He has very decided ideas on death and all that it means.

He is the only person I have met who seems to have large ideas about the universe, and I want to hear much more about them and to listen to him.

I feel one ought to think about the world one lives in, and—though I have laughed at Ivor for it—about humanity.

When I am in Grosvenor Square nothing seems to matter very much, except having a lovely time and being admired, and looking pretty.

But when I am with Ivor I feel that the world and the people in it, and even the nation itself, matter terribly, and every one of us can try to do something to improve and better the things around us.

Ivor is always talking about helping the individual, but somehow his ideas are not half so individualistic as those of my other friends.

Though he talks for the individual, he seems to think collectively, while in Grosvenor Square it is the other way about.

Everyone seems to be thinking just of himself and of nothing outside.

Anyway, I do want Ivor to get well, and please God, don't let him die!

REFLECTION THIRTY-FOUR

This is an extraordinary party.

At the moment our host is singing, pretty badly, to a ukulele, and everyone seems to be behaving in a very odd manner; this is the amount of vodka most of them have drunk, I think.

I do not think Uncle Lionel would approve of this, but it isn't Aunt Dorothy's fault that I am here.

After all, Timmy rang up this morning to suggest that he should give a dinner-party for us at the Embassy, and then we would all go on to Jackie Denton's party.

Denton owns a lot of racehorses; everybody knows him, and everybody calls him 'Jackie'.

I think he is rather nice but some of his friends are most peculiar.

Aunt Dorothy did hesitate for a moment before she accepted for me, because she could not accept Timmy's invitation herself. But as there were three married women in the party, they ought to be enough chaperonage, she said, and I could go.

We did have a very amusing dinner.

The other men of the party are not so very young, except Rossy, who has squeezed himself in somehow.

This charade is too impossible. I cannot understand a

word they are saying. It seems to me that they must be all rather drunk, or pretending to be.

The acting seems to consist of messing about; the girls are kissed a good deal, and they are all dressed up in everybody's hats and coats, and looked quite fantastic.

Everyone else seems to think it very funny. I do feel so priggish and stupid not to be really amused.

Of course, I am pretending to laugh, but all this falling about and kissing, and this frightful noise, does not strike me as being so terribly funny as all that.

I think I will go home ... but I am sure Timmy will be offended if I do.

There is a telephone bell ringing somewhere, but no one seems to answer it.

Isn't it queer how a telephone note sounds above everything else?—I suppose it is because it is so shrill.

*   *   *   *

I wonder if we shall be there in time—I cannot bear to think we shan't.

Ivor dying! ... It cannot be true!

I wish to goodness this man would drive faster, he's so terribly slow.

Ivor dying ... Poppy could not have meant it ... She sounded very agitated, but I could hardly hear what she said with the awful noise of that damn silly party.

Oh ... hurry! Hurry! ... Why must there be traffic in the streets at this hour?

Oh ... please don't let Ivor die! Please, God, don't let him die before I get there! ...

It is funny how one never realises how fond one is of somebody until one is likely to lose them. I had no idea I loved Ivor so much ... Dear Ivor! Always fighting the world ... always so upset with the condition of everything!

How I wish this car would go quicker!

It comforts me somehow to hold Rossy's hand—I feel I must hold on to something.

I am not crying ... I feel sort of numb, only agitated

inside, because I want to push this car quicker and quicker . . . I wish I could fly . . .

Oh, don't let him die . . . he cannot die before I get there! . . .

Rossy has not said a word since we started. I think that is rather understanding of him. I simply cannot talk . . . I could not bear anyone to say they were sorry.

Here is Sloane Square . . . thank goodness we have got as far as this.

Oh, damn that taxi . . . why must it get in the way?

Hurry . . . hurry . . . I must get there!

Please, God, don't let him die . . . don't let him die! He must get well . . . he is so young . . . why should he die?

It is so unfair . . . he is not doing any harm in the world, and there cannot possibly be any point or reason in his life ending so soon.

Hurry . . . hurry! We are nearly there . . . Here's the street at last . . .

Oh, God, please let him be alive when I see him! . . .

REFLECTION THIRTY-FIVE

It is over a week since Ivor died, and I have not somehow been able to take an interest in anything.

It isn't as though I used to see an awful lot of him, but still he has left an enormous gap, a sort of hole in my life, or, rather, my feelings, I suppose.

He was so alive, so interested, so intense about everything, it seems impossible that I shall never see him again!

It is so silly, and I suppose it is nerves, but when I go out every man I see walking along seems for a second to remind me of Ivor.

I keep thinking ... almost before I think ... that I see him.

I can quite understand people going into mourning when they are fond of somebody. I have felt as though I could not face a bright-coloured dress.

It's silly, because I think that Ivor would have hated me to wear black for him. He'd have thought it a lot of outward show and circumstance which had nothing to do with one's real feelings.

Of course, it has not really—and yet one seems to do it to express the depression one is feeling in oneself.

And Poppy is here with me.

Uncle Lionel was terribly nice. He came down the next morning after that terrible night. I still cannot think of

Ivor dying, without feeling rather sick, it was all so horrible, so terrible to watch.

I do not think he knew me, but I am glad I was there.

Rossy was very kind—I think it shook him, rather.

I shall never forget the doctor drawing back the curtains after he was dead, and the very early sun coming in at the window. It seemed wrong, somehow, that sun ... almost blasphemous on top of what had happened.

Poor Poppy! I know now that I was right, and that she did love Ivor.

Uncle Lionel was wonderful, and arranged the funeral and everything. And Ivor's parents—I saw them for a moment. They were rather pathetic, really, and I think perhaps Ivor had been rather hard on them.

However, it is Poppy who matters, and Uncle Lionel is so much better with her than I am. He just insisted on her staying here for the time being.

I've cried so much this last week that I think my eyes will be permanently swollen.

I'd better bathe them, and lie down for a little bit.

... Yes—I think I will wear my white lace.

REFLECTION THIRTY-SIX

The most lovely, thrilling thing—I have had a cable from Tommy!

I am so frightfully pleased, and feel as if I were on tiptoe with excitement.

Ages and ages ago I wrote to Tommy, when I was in Chelsea, and told him I had run away from home. And then, when I came back, I sent him a tiny note to say I had returned to the fold.

He never answered my first letter, and I was very hurt that he had not, and felt something must have happened to it—and of course he had never got it, because he was away.

And the cable:

Found both your letters at studio. Have just returned from Morocco. Arriving London to-morrow. Staying Claridge's. Love. Tommy.

It will be too marvellous to see him again!

He was always so very sweet, and so attractive. I do hope he will think I have improved in looks.

He has not stayed away the year that he talked about, but perhaps three months is enough.

I am simply longing to see him again, and I do wish Thelma was coming with him.

I wonder if he will think me attractive. I cannot help thinking, just secretly to myself, that perhaps Tommy will be in love with me, and that I shall be in love with him.

I think he always has been at the back of my mind. I am sure that really I have thought about him lots and lots since I last saw him.

It would be rather wonderful if he made love to me, and I loved him. Perhaps we might even get married! It would be so terribly romantic to marry someone who had loved you since you were a schoolgirl.

If he thought I was attractive then, in those perfectly frightful clothes, I am sure he will think me lovely now, because I have improved a lot—I can see it myself.

I was terribly inane, and had nothing to talk about or to say in those days, and now all sorts of people seem to find me amusing, so I am sure Tommy will.

I do hope he has not loved anybody else since I last saw him.

Of course, looking back, I did not know when I left Paris that he loved me, but I think now that he must have.

After all, he quite obviously wanted to kiss me, and said he would come and tell me why I was 'unsettling' in a year's time.

I shall insist on his telling me now, anyway, and I don't suppose that he himself wants to wait a year.

It will really be rather a snub for Alec, and of course Rossy, and all the other people, if I marry Tommy. I should like to tell them that I had loved him all the time—that was why their charms had failed to attract me.

Not that Harry would mind whom I marry, but still he seems to interfere with anyone whom I want to, but I expect that is only to pay me out for knowing about him and Aunt Dorothy.

Aunt Dorothy's new young man is really very nice.

He has lent me two of his polo ponies to ride whenever I like, and he keeps Aunt Dorothy in such a good temper that the atmosphere about the house is quite heavenly these days.

Poppy has got a job at last—Uncle Lionel got it for her.

It's a secretary's job of sorts, to some old man he knows at the House, and Poppy is frightfully pleased about it.

She won't live here any more, but in a tiny flat in Westminster. Uncle Lionel insisted on giving her all the furnishing for it, and would not allow her to refuse.

She is terribly happy, and I see a lot of her. She comes and talks to me while I am dressing for dinner in the evening, when her work is done.

I must tell Tommy all about Ivor and Poppy. Of course he will be thrilled, because I wrote him quite a lot about them when I was in Chelsea.

I do wish he could have met Ivor—and I think Ivor would have liked Tommy the best of all my friends.

In fact, I am sure he would, because Tommy of course is artistic too, and awfully outspoken and against all sort of pretence, just like Ivor—only Ivor was more violent about it perhaps.

Shall I meet Tommy at Claridge's, or shall I wait for him to come down here? I think I'll meet him at Claridge's.

I want him to see me just as myself, without any surroundings, or anything. I am sure he will be awfully surprised at how I have altered.

I shall wear my new blue *crêpe-de-Chine*—it makes me look awfully sophisticated, I think, and I want to look very grown-up and tremendously *chic*, not a schoolgirl any more.

I am so excited about everything, and I do think it would be rather lovely to marry Tommy and live in Paris and London. And we could make trips to New York to see his father.

We would always spend the season in London, and we could go to the south, or Morocco, or one of those places that Tommy likes so much in the cold weather.

With Tommy's and my money we should be tremendously rich, and that would be rather fun.

No one could possibly say that Tommy was marrying me for my money, because he will one day, I suppose, own all his father's business in America.

Oh, I can hardly wait for to-morrow, I am so excited about all this!

Shall I cable him, I wonder, that I will meet him—or

not? No, I don't think so—I will just wait for him in the entrance hall, and if he does not recognise me, how marvellous it would be!

I would just walk about, looking awfully smart, and then, if he took no notice of me, I could say:

"Don't you know who I am?"

And he'd say:

"Good heavens, it's Maxine! You are so lovely, and so awfully *chic*, I did not recognise you!"

That really would be a wonderful way to start! Oh—I must do that!

I do wish it was to-morrow—I shan't sleep a wink to-night, planning things.

REFLECTION THIRTY-SEVEN

I do think it is a pity that people cannot be made always to wear a label describing who they are.

Like a ticket for Ascot and the Royal enclosure, only with more details added.

Of course, I know that Tommy is awfully distinguished, and that he has made a name for himself in Paris as an artist, but it is difficult in London to explain that people wear peculiar clothes because they are artistic.

He is very tall, and nice-looking in an American sort of way, but nevertheless I do think it is a pity to make people stare.

Of course I know they are people who do not matter, and who have done nothing in the world except manage to get born into Society.

But, anyway, they are 'Society', however they wangled their birth, and I may be very weak-minded, but I do dislike criticism of my friends.

I wish I was the sort of person who could really and truly not care what people say about me or about the people of whom I am fond.

Anyway, I really mind very much that Tommy will wear such peculiar and artistic ties, and such extraordinary odd suits.

I'd quite forgotten, too, that he had such a strong American accent.

It's awfully difficult to judge somebody when you haven't seen them for a long time and have seen a totally different crowd of people in between.

My first thought on seeing Tommy was how un-English he looked, and in spite of all my plans about myself, and the hours I'd spent dressing, he recognised me at once and said:

"Hullo, Maxine! You are just the same—you haven't altered a scrap."

And I did think that was too disappointing, as I'd blackened my eyelashes and made my mouth simply crimson.

He wore an enormous travelling coat, and a black hat with a huge brim, and he looked so unlike Harry or Alec or any of the men I know well, that if anybody I knew had come into Claridge's just then I know they would have said:

"Who is that quite extraordinary man talking to Maxine?"

Of course, I know it's very stupid, and that those things—I mean clothes—don't count at all in friendship.

But still, I did have that feeling, although of course I was as pleased as anything to see Tommy, and could simply have hugged him.

But I did not, because I was trying to be grown-up and awfully sophisticated.

He did not kiss my hand, like he did when he said good-bye, but just shook it very hard. We went and had a cocktail together, and talked and talked—at least, I talked, and told him all about myself.

It is only now I realise how very little of Tommy's life I know anything about—just that he paints, and that Thelma is his sister.

Though I had meant to tell Tommy all that had happened in my life, and make him a sort of father confessor, now that I have seen him I somehow don't want to.

The funny thing is, I don't think Tommy is in love with me after all; at least, not properly in love.

He paid me quite a lot of compliments, and I asked him if my face was still 'unsettling'.

He grinned, and said:

"I shall have to find that out, and will let you know in a day or two."

I saw that he really thought it was, but still there was not anything more to it, it all seemed rather on the surface.

And though we have been about together in the last few days, I don't seem to have got to know him any better.

He thinks most of my friends are awful, which is so upsetting. He does not like Mona at all. I thought they would get on quite well. I asked him why he did not like her, and he said:

"When I want someone to pose I pay for it."

Aunt Dorothy did not think much of him—I could tell that. Of course, she was charming: she always is to young men. But I knew she was surprised at his clothes and at his American expressions.

When I was in Paris, I did not think that Tommy talked American at all—at least, only occasionally, when he was annoyed, but now to me it seems very pronounced.

I suppose it's after living among English voices for so long.

He dined last night, and we went to a party. Aunt Dorothy took us, of course. Half way through the evening he said:

"I simply cannot stand this any longer, Maxine—I'll ring you to-morrow."

And he walked out before I could even protest.

That's rather rude, I do think when I've gone out of my way to amuse him, and tried to introduce him to all sorts of people. Anyway, it made the party short of a man, and that is unpardonable.

This decides one thing, however—that I was quite, quite wrong in thinking that one day I might marry Tommy.

REFLECTION THIRTY-EIGHT

I came in rather late from my ride yesterday morning.

It was such a lovely day, and I was enjoying it so much, that, although I remembered an appointment with Tommy, I thought it would not do him any harm to wait for me.

I do hope I am not getting conceited, but I do think that he treats me rather casually considering that everyone else is so awfully nice and attentive to me.

He just arranges things if he feels like it, and if not he does not ring up at all. I waited the whole afternoon the other day, expecting him to come round and see me, and he never rang up until just before dinner.

"Where have you been?" I said.

"Oh, I've been sightseeing," he replied. "I started off this morning, and got around in the docks, and I have been there ever since making sketches."

I was furious, because I'd wasted hours and hours waiting for him, and he might easily have telephoned me. There must be a telephone somewhere at the docks.

I did not hurry home, but went on riding in the sunshine, and enjoying myself. And I had a very charming companion—an excuse in itself.

He is in the Brigade, and said the nicest things about the way I rode, and what good hands I'd got.

157

And when I did get back it was nearly a quarter to one, and I saw Tommy's hat in the hall.

I do wish he'd wear a normal-sized brim, but it's no use talking to him, he's so pig-headed, and says that sort is comfortable and he has always worn it.

I ran into the morning-room, and there was Tommy talking to Poppy, who had come from Westminster with some papers for Uncle Lionel from the old man for whom she works.

They both said "Hullo!" but they did not seem as though they had missed me very much, or even worried that I was late.

So I went up to change, and when I came down they had gone! Really too extraordinary, because Tommy was lunching with me at the Ritz.

I rang up Poppy's office to ask what had happened, but she had not got back yet, and then at nearly half past one Tommy arrived, quite casually, with no apologies.

He had walked to Westminster with Poppy.

"I thought you'd take hours changing," he said.

I was rather acid about being kept waiting, but I really was rather cross, because that sort of thing is needlessly rude from a man to a girl.

So I was very cold all through lunch, but he did not seem to notice at all, but went on talking about the sketches he was making, and how he had never realised before how many interesting things there were in London.

He said he intended to stay here for ages and go on making sketches for pictures which he would complete when he went back to Paris.

If he is going to stay as long as that, I really think there is no reason for me to fuss about him. He ought to be able to look after himself and make his own friends.

Of course, I shall always be pleased to see him, because I am very fond of Tommy and Thelma, but I really cannot be kept waiting all the time, or left without an explanation, by any man, however artistic he may be.

I must say it is all rather amusing, though, because the first two or three days Tommy was here everybody raised their eyebrows and looked most surprised when they saw him with me.

They asked who he was in the most condescending sort of way.

Then the gossip papers came out with pages about him and his works, saying how brilliant he was and that he had started a new school of painting, and that he was the son of a millionaire and that Thelma was the most beautiful *débutante* in America.

Then everyone became so interested, and lots of people rang me up and asked me to bring Tommy round to lunch or dinner.

At first I thought this was rather fun, but when Tommy would not go, and I had to make excuses—polite ones which he would not even help to invent—it ceased to be a joke.

Lady Ardnick, Aunt Dorothy's friend, has rung up at least ten times.

Tommy says nothing would induce him to go to any of her luncheon parties because he has known about her for years, and he has always made up his mind to avoid her.

She collects 'lions' and her luncheon parties are too awful because everyone is a 'lion', and so brilliant that there is no audience. They never listen to each other, but just sit waiting for an opportunity to speak.

The result is, everyone is bored and annoyed, and Tommy says:

"If one must be a lion, one must roar alone, and not in unison."

And I said I wished he'd explain this to Lady Ardnick, because I am so tired of inventing excuses on the telephone.

Now I have even had to get Miss Roberts to say I am out if she telephones again, or else I shall put her straight on to Tommy himself.

One thing, however, is extraordinary—very; that Tommy and Harry are friends. I am awfully surprised.

We were all lunching at Quaglino's—Aunt Dorothy and Ronald, Tommy and myself, and Baba and Derek, who had just returned from a weekend in the country.

Harry was sitting at the next table with two men, and when he saw Aunt Dorothy he came to our table and spoke to her.

"Hullo!" he said when he saw Tommy.

159

They shook hands and were awfully pleased to see each other.

They have met lots of times in Paris, and, judging by the reminiscences and the joking which went on, I should think that some of the parties they attended there together must have been very peculiar.

I wonder that Tommy, who is supposed to be so clever, could bother with the sort of parties which Harry seems to think amusing.

I did not speak to him, but just stared right through him and talked to Ronald instead.

When he went away, Tommy said to me:

"Now there's a charming man. Why aren't you friends with him, instead of some of the riff-raff I've met you with?"

And I said I was glad he thought he was charming—perhaps he did not know him as well as I did.

"Nonsense, Maxine. I have known him for over five years, and he is a very good sort," Tommy said.

I should have thought that Harry was the last person Tommy would have liked, or that Harry would have liked Tommy. So it just shows you never can tell another person's tastes in the way of friends.

But I am really very disappointed in Tommy, because I did think we should have an amusing time together.

And another thing which annoys me very much is that I always thought that, as I knew him so well, he would tell me about Alec, and why they were all so peculiar about him.

But when I told him the whole story, instead of being surprised or horrified, Tommy just laughed and laughed.

And I was frightfully angry, but he only said:

"I am only surprised it does not happen oftener to you poor little rich girls! Anyhow, I think it would have been better to tell you the truth instead of making such a mystery about it, and that would teach you to keep away from 'nice boys'!"

And he said 'nice boys' with such an affected accent.

I do not quite understand what Tommy was trying to tell me, because he was just as garbled and silly about it all as everyone else had been.

But I did gather one thing—that Harry was quite right

160

to tell Uncle Lionel, so perhaps it was silly of me to have been quite so angry with Harry.

I am rather glad he was right, and that it was not just nastiness on his part, as I thought.

But still, if he had been sensible, and tried to explain to me that Alec belonged to a kind of sect—it sounds like a religion, or something of that sort—of course I should have understood.

Instead of which he tore about and made such a scene that naturally I was furious.

I do think it makes life very difficult if people are peculiar like that and you don't know it, while people like Harry and Tommy know it.

It would be so much better if they wore a badge, or something, so that one could know at once, and then no mistakes could be made.

REFLECTION THIRTY-NINE

What an extraordinary thing to happen; and I really am very pleased about it!

Tommy and Poppy are going to be married!

It is all very romantic and exciting, and I feel a sort of fairy godmother for having brought them together.

And it all happened at that lovely little house on the river which Aunt Dorothy always takes in the summer so that she can get away from London for week-ends.

We have not been down there before, there has been so much to do, and the weather at week-ends has been foul.

But last Saturday was perfectly lovely, and down we went, and sat in the garden and went up the river in punts.

It was Uncle Lionel who suggested that Poppy should come too, which was very sweet of him, because she has been working so hard, and still isn't very strong after Ivor's death.

Aunt Dorothy said I could ask a man, and I thought of course I ought to ask Tommy, otherwise I might have invited Rossy.

Tommy accepted, and Aunt Dorothy asked Mona and a very nice young man whom she likes, and of course Ronald—Aunt Dorothy's friend.

There was another married woman, who I imagine was

asked to amuse Uncle Lionel, but I do not think he likes her very much, as she was really rather tiresome.

She would stay in bed until lunch-time and then wanted to stay up all night playing backgammon, which is a game I detest—I always lose!

We had great fun, and I did notice that Tommy was very pleased with Poppy.

They kept disappearing in a punt—he said he'd gone up the river to make sketches, but I had a look at his sketch-book, and he had not drawn a single stroke, except a drawing of Poppy's head.

And that seemed to me to be very little work to have done during the whole day if he was sketching as hard as he said he was, but I was very tactful, and said nothing.

That is one thing I've learnt during the last months—not to make remarks about anything people do.

I was always doing that when I first came out, and Aunt Dorothy used to get simply furious and glare at me, and so did the people I was talking about.

Now I am so well trained that I know if I saw people quite naked upside-down in the passage I should take no notice, but say, 'excuse me,' and pass on!

After dinner on Saturday night we danced and Tommy and Poppy disappeared into the garden. It was a very dark night, lots of stars but no moon.

They took the electric canoe, and went up the river. I was alone and then Uncle Lionel came on to the veranda and said to me:

"Your young man deserting you, Maxine?"

And I laughed and said:

"I don't think he's my young man any more! Do you, Uncle Lionel?"

"I think they suit each other rather well," he said. "I like your little friend Poppy, and she knows a lot about life and men, and you need a great deal of knowledge if you are going to tackle an artistic man. An artistic woman's difficult enough, Maxine, but an artistic man is the devil!"

I slipped my arm into his, and we went for a walk about the garden.

Uncle Lionel really is very nice. He knows a lot about

life, and sees far more of what is going on than most people imagine.

"How many times have you been in love, Uncle Lionel?" I asked him.

"Thousands of times, my dear—I've forgotten to count them."

"Have you ever had a great big enormous love," I said, "that mattered more than anything else in the world, and which you could never forget?"

"All love is like that when it is happening, Maxine, and if it does not feel like that to one it is not worth having. But when it's over you cannot remember what it felt like until the next one comes along.

"I know you have been reading novels," he went on, "reading about people sacrificing their whole life for one love, or perhaps it is the cinema that has taught you that. It's nonsense, believe me.

"I've lived a good many years, and, although there are exceptions to every rule, I assure you I have found that the average person loves a good many times in their life, and each of their loves can be as intense as the other.

"Of course if somebody dies, or leaves them before their love has burnt itself out, they always imagine that it was the love of their lifetime, and idealize it, simply because they themselves are left unsatisfied.

"But real love, thank God, can come again and again."

I have determined that I shall have lots and lots of talks with Uncle Lionel, because I am sure he can tell me such a heap of things I do not know.

I shall have to inveigle him into talking with me, because when I said that to him I remember he laughed and said:

"No one learns by anyone else's experience, Maxine. I could talk to you until to-morrow morning, and you still would not have learnt half as much from me as you would in five minutes from a man you were in love with."

After a while we went back to the house. Aunt Dorothy was still dancing to the gramophone with Ronald, and Mona with her young man.

The other woman was screaming for someone to come and play backgammon with her.

I cannot think why Aunt Dorothy likes dancing so

much. I do hope I shan't when I am her age. She simply loves it, and is furious if her young men don't dance just the way she wants them to.

Uncle Lionel and I were trying to decide who should play with the awful woman.

We tossed up when she was not looking, and of course I lost, so I had to, and she beat me, and I had to give her ten shillings.

It began to get very late, I think it was about one o'clock, and Aunt Dorothy said, "Let's go to bed."

And we were just going to when Tommy and Poppy came in, and I saw at once that something had happened, because Poppy was looking absolutely radiant, and really very pretty.

She is not pretty as a rule, just rather quaint-looking, but when she came into the drawing-room into the light she really looked lovely.

Tommy followed her, and he seemed more ordinary, but sort of affectedly so, as though he was acting. He poured himself out a drink.

It was Aunt Dorothy who asked:

"You two children enjoyed yourselves?"

"Yes, it's nice up the river," Tommy replied in a very obviously casual voice.

When we got upstairs she came to my room and told "What's happened?"

"We're engaged," she said, "don't tell the others yet."

When we got upstairs she came to my room and told me all about it, and how frightfully happy she was.

She had told Tommy all about her friend, the married man, and he did not mind a bit.

I am glad she told him, because I could not help thinking quickly in my mind, when she first said she was engaged, that it would be awful if her romance began like a kind of cinema story, where the heroine is always terrified about her husband finding out about her past.

All the same, I think it was very brave of her to tell Tommy, because he might have been horrified and refused to marry her.

But he did not mind a bit, and they are going to get married very soon and go to Tommy's studio in Paris.

The only thing that is very disappointing is that they won't be married in a Church, but in a Registry Office.

I begged Poppy to have a Church and white satin and orange blossom wedding, because I do think that all that is so exciting, and one can only have it once in one's life.

"Neither Tommy nor I believe in all that," she said.

I do hope that Poppy and Tommy are terribly happy together, and I think they will be, because Poppy won't mind Tommy's erratic moods a bit.

If he does not turn up for an appointment she won't worry like I should, but just be pleased to see him when he does arrive.

She's awfully pleased at having to give up her job. She said she hated the stereotypedness of it, and always having to be in the same place at the same time.

She is going to continue with her drawing in Paris, but she says she thinks it will be almost a whole-time job looking after Tommy.

She's very likely right.

REFLECTION FORTY

Poppy and Tommy were married yesterday morning at the Chelsea Registry Office.

I have never seen a more depressing place, but they were so awfully happy, and didn't seem to mind. I was one witness, and Harry was the other.

They got married at about twelve o'clock, so it wasn't so very early, and I insisted on Poppy letting me give her a wedding dress, which was really very pretty, of bright lacquer red georgette, with a coat to match trimmed with grey fox.

Tommy gave her a spray of orchids, white ones with little red spots on them, which were very unusual and attractive.

When we first arrived, we sat for ages on hard chairs in a pea-green distempered room.

Then the Registrar came in, and of course he had a cold and snuffled through his nose; but they repeated everything after him, and in about two seconds they were married.

Poppy and Tommy were radiantly happy, and quite absurd. They just looked at each other, and smiled and said nothing, and smiled again.

Aunt Dorothy, who really turned up trumps over the whole thing, gave an enormous luncheon for them at

Grosvenor Square, and Poppy asked all her old friends to come.

They did look so odd mixed up with some of Aunt Dorothy's friends and Tommy's. It was all very gay and informal and amusing, because the luncheon wasn't a proper sit-down one.

The dining-room was filled with tiny tables to seat four or six, so everybody sat where they liked and talked and laughed, and there was lots of champagne.

We had lunch early, because they were going to catch the 1.50 to Paris.

I went with them to the station to see them off, and we threw lots of rice, and photographers took masses of photographs, which came out in all the evening papers, and they wrote up all sorts of rubbish about 'Romance in Artistic Circles'.

There were photographs of me too, and Aunt Dorothy and Uncle Lionel—though they did not seem to have much to do with it—and of course Harry, I suppose, as best man.

I have never seen Poppy look so lovely.

It does seem as though love makes beauties out of quite plain people, so if you were very beautiful already, goodness knows what it would do to you!

I gave Poppy a very pretty sapphire and diamond brooch, and Uncle Lionel gave her earrings to match it, which was awfully sweet of him.

Tommy did not give her an ordinary-looking engagement ring at all, but an enormous cabochon emerald, carved into a quite peculiar shape. It was really rather attractive, and suited Poppy's rather strange appearance.

I helped Poppy get some of her clothes, and insisted on paying for them, although of course she was pig-headed, and would not let me do half I wanted to. But I said she really could not marry Tommy with no clothes at all, and she had practically nothing that was not in rags.

In the end she gave in, but she swore she would pay me back with every drawing she sells.

When they had left Victoria and the train had steamed out of the station, and we had waved until they were quite out of sight, I found myself going back in a car with Harry alone.

I don't know quite how it happened, but all the others seemed to have got into the cars in front, and I was the last to be left waiting.

As the car actually drove out of Victoria station I tried hard to think of my little speech to say I was sorry.

But there was no need for it, because Harry put out his hand and said:

"What about it, Maxine?"

I put my hand into his, and we just smiled at each other and everything was all right.

I am so very glad that we are friends again, because it really is so boring having rows with people, especially when you like them very much.

I do like Harry so awfully, and he is such a wonderful person when he wants to be.

So that makes everything all right, and I do hope that Tommy and Poppy are very happy. I wonder if it would be very embarrassing to be alone with somebody just after you married them.

It seems to me there would be very little to say, but I suppose I am quite wrong, and one would really have lots to talk about.

But it must be very strange to think:

"I now belong to this man, and of course he belongs to me."

I'm not certain I should not be awfully frightened, and want to rush away, but of course it depends on whom one marries, and if you know them very well; and I do not think Poppy will ever want to run away from Tommy.

What is so lovely is that Tommy admires her most awfully, and wants to paint a picture of her. It must be terrible if your husband loves you very much, but still thinks you are not as pretty as all the other women he knows.

Of course, that must happen to lots of people, because quite plain women get married, and yet they seem very happy.

Naturally it is not only to do with looks, but I would want my husband to admire me very much.

I wonder if Harry thinks I am pretty. I hope he does, but of course I am not a bit the same type as Aunt Dorothy.

Mona says that all men admire the same type, and that

if a man marries for the second time he always marries a woman who looks exactly like his first wife.

In which case Harry could not admire me very much, except in an aloof way, or something like that, because Aunt Dorothy is so tiny, and dark, and I am ever so much taller than she is.

Still, I am glad my skin is so white, even in the mornings, and some people like red hair very much indeed.

I wonder if it will get darker as I get older?

REFLECTION FORTY-ONE

I can hardly believe it, but Mona is in love with Harry!

I was absolutely stupefied when I heard it. It really is too absurd, the way girls find him so attractive, and apparently married women too.

I remember hearing that he never looked at a girl, but of course Mona does seem like a young married woman, because she is so sophisticated.

So he may like her better than anyone else.

I can't understand it, because though she's pretty, and awfully smart, she's not so very clever, or anything like that, and I should have thought that Harry would have liked clever women.

Mona told me that she was terribly fond of him, and when she first told me I nearly said:

"Well, you have not got much hope, anyway!"

Luckily I didn't, before she added that he had taken her out quite a lot lately.

Then I was more surprised than ever, because that seems very unlike Harry.

I do not believe they have been out as much as Mona pretended; nevertheless, she would not lie about the whole thing, and so there obviously must be some truth in the story.

I would like to know if he's really fond of her, or just passing the time.

After all, he has been about with Aunt Dorothy for so long that he must find he has a lot of empty evenings and time to spare, in spite of being so popular.

Mona says that now the season is ending they are all making plans to go to the South of France, and she thinks that Harry is going to join their party.

I cannot understand it—I cannot really.

What can he see in Mona?

I suppose she is pretty, though I don't know that I admire her type very much myself, and of course lots of people laugh at her way of dressing and the way she talks.

The papers write her up a good deal as 'the smartest and most beautiful *débutante* of her year'.

Still, papers can be wrong—and it just surprises me, that's all, that Harry should admire her.

I wish I could see Harry again—I would love to have a talk with him about things.

But if he is thinking of marrying and settling down—and I expect Mona would marry him at once, if he asked her—it would be quite useless to be friends with him again.

I wonder if I could possibly run into him accidentally, and have a little talk. It oughtn't to be difficult.

There don't seem any very exciting parties this next week. Two *débutante* balls, one small supper-dance with the same collection of giggling fools, and one dinner-party for a first night.

He won't be at any of those.

Of course he might go to one with Mona, but according to her they have been going out alone.

I really don't know what her mother is thinking of, except I suppose she would be delighted if Mona did marry Harry, because he is a big catch.

I never realised until the other day that his family was so old and so very distinguished, and that his house in Warwickshire is perfectly lovely, and quite famous, and the Standish jewels are often exhibited, because they are unique.

Mona would enjoy wearing them. She loves jewellery,

172

and I suppose she would wear the emerald tiara to be presented at Court.

I wonder if Harry really intends to marry her? I do wish I could see him.

Of course he's wonderfully good-looking—not in a striking way, but really good-looking, sort of English. It sounds frightful! But that's really what one thinks of—that very clean, big look.

Will he be playing polo today? I might ask Aunt Dorothy if I could have the car and go to Ranelagh. I am sure I could get one of my girl friends to go with me.

I'll go and ask Aunt Dorothy.

REFLECTION FORTY-TWO

Aunt Dorothy, some of her friends, Rossy and I went to a party in the River Room at the Savoy last night and when we were leaving we went upstairs past the restaurant.

Walking into the hall I bumped into Harry and Mona.

They said, "Hello!" and we all chattered and moved towards the entrance together.

I think I must have quite lost my head, or else it was because Mona looked so smug at being with Harry, and so very pleased with herself.

But I dropped behind a tiny bit from the others, and manoeuvred myself next to Harry, and said:

"I want to see you—it's very important."

"Of course, Maxine," he said. "Is anything the matter?"—quickly and rather seriously.

"I cannot tell you now," I said, "but will you please ring me up tomorrow?"

"Of course I will," he said. "Good-night, my dear, don't worry."

And now I've done it, and I cannot think of anything to say to him when he does ring up!

I've been so worried at the thought of having said what I did, with no real reason, that I've been awake since seven o'clock.

I don't suppose for one moment that Harry will telephone me before ten, for he knows how late we all sleep in this household.

What on earth am I going to say when he does ring me up?

I dare say it was quite wrong of me to suggest it, but it was so infuriating to see Mona so pleased with herself for being with him.

Really, I think it's perfectly absurd for a girl of her age to wear such low backs, and to make her face up as much as she does.

Personally I should have thought that any man would think it quite ludicrous, but apparently Harry doesn't.

I still cannot think of anything to say. It really makes me look such a fool, begging him to ring me up like that, and then being without an excuse.

What shall I say? I must think of something.

Heavens! There's the telephone now . . .

REFLECTION FORTY-THREE

Oh, I've had the most lovely, wonderful day ... with Harry!

He did not ask for any explanation on the telephone at all, which made things so much easier.

"Are you doing anything today?" he said.

I said no at once, because I thought he was going to ask me to do something—and he did!

He suggested that we should go into the country in his car, and lunch at some funny little pub or other.

Of course I was thrilled, and flung on some clothes—and had to wait ages when I was dressed, because he said he would be round in an hour, and I was dressed in about ten minutes.

He came round in his lovely Bentley, driving himself and I left a message for Aunt Dorothy that I had gone out to lunch.

I did not say who with, because I thought she would be so surprised, and it was only after we'd started that I remembered a collection of my friends were coming to lunch!

We did not say very much at first, but just drove along in the sunshine in silence. It was all so lovely, and I felt suddenly so very happy.

Harry is most awfully nice, and if Mona does marry

him she will be the luckiest girl in the whole world. But somehow I've a funny feeling inside me that she won't.

We drove on and on into the most wonderful country in Surrey, and then he took me to lunch at a little wayside pub.

There was hardly anybody there, but we had the most delicious lunch—I cannot remember what it was, but I know that I enjoyed it very much.

We talked and talked about everything and everybody, and what we felt about things.

I said to him:

"You know I've made lots of silly mistakes, and done very silly things since I've come out, but I do think it's a good thing to make them quickly, and get them over. I could not bear to make mistakes which I went on trying to justify for years and years."

But before this, of course, we had made up our row.

"You're not angry with me any more, Maxine?" Harry asked.

"No, let's forget about it," I answered.

He knew by what I'd said about mistakes, that I was referring to Alec, and that I knew I'd made a fool of myself.

Because he said, very seriously:

"We all of us make mistakes, Maxine, and damn silly ones at that. But I am certain that they can always be rectified if one tries. Don't you think so?"

I said I was sure they could, but of course one had to be careful not to make the same silly mistake again.

"By that, I suppose," he said, "you are referring to getting mixed up with silly people."

I said yes, and that I was certain all of us were too inclined to take people as we found them, and not to delve deep enough into their true characters.

I know it was horribly catty of me, but I could not help saying this rather meaningly, and thinking there were lots of things about Mona which it would be better for him to find out before he married her.

I know one thing which I'm sure would horrify Harry—at least, I imagine it would—and that is that Mona does not want to have any children.

I must say I have not thought about it very much, but I know I would like to have them—I adore babies.

If I had them, I would like their father to be very English and good-looking, and rather serious-minded too.

One could not bring children into the world with a father who thought about nothing but night clubs and tearing about, like Rossy, for instance, or Timmy.

I think that if Harry settled down he would make a perfect father, and of course one would always be awfully proud if one's children looked like him.

Perhaps he does not mind, and Mona has already told him how she feels about things like that, but if I had a wonderful historic home I should want to have a son to inherit it.

After luncheon we went on in the car till we came to some wonderful woods, and we sat under the trees and Harry smoked a cigarette.

We talked about all sorts of things. Harry has terribly nice ideas on everything.

I know one thing—if I am sincere with myself—I love Harry more than ever. And yet I don't think I've ever stopped loving him since the first time I saw him.

He's always been there, in my thoughts, though I've tried terribly hard to forget about him. I do wish we never had this silly row, and that we could go back to the night that he kissed me.

But he has never said anything about kissing me again, or even paid me a compliment.

But I think he enjoyed our day, and that he was happy with me. I know I was terribly happy with him.

We got back just before dinner, and I don't think I've ever had a more wonderful time.

The awful thing is that the season is coming to an end, and everyone is going away. If Harry goes to the South of France I shan't see him for months and months.

We are going to stay with friends, Aunt Dorothy and I, in all sorts of places, and she has not said a word about going to the South, although we may go to Paris for a short time.

Harry must not get engaged to Mona before he comes back to London.

But it is no use worrying; I shall see him again to-morrow, because he is going to meet me in the Row in the morning, when I ride.

I do love Harry ... I do, more than anybody in the world!

This is quite a different love from anything else I felt for the other people, because my love for him has been inside me all the time.

I think it has been growing, in spite of my being angry with him and everything.

I feel quite, quite different from the way I felt for the other silly people.

I do wonder what Harry feels about me.

REFLECTION FORTY-FOUR

I am so angry, I can hardly think, and it's all over that little beast Mona.

I arranged to meet Harry this morning and I was looking forward to it more than anything in the world. So I arrived in the Row very punctually, and found the groom waiting with my horse, but there was no sign of Harry.

So I fiddled about a little bit to give him plenty of time, I altered the girths, and talked to the groom.

Then, about ten minutes late, Harry drives up in his Bentley, and who should be sitting beside him but Mona!

Of course I've seen her in the Row once or twice, but she has told me that secretly she dislikes riding, and it's such a bother to get up before luncheon, and of course no one rides in the afternoon.

So I knew she had only come out today so as to be with Harry, and I should not be a bit surprised if she hadn't known I was going to be there, and determined to do me down.

She had borrowed one of Harry's polo ponies as well, for his groom arrived with his horse, and the pony for her.

I must confess—though at that moment I disliked her more than I have ever disliked anyone—that she looks very well in riding things.

She was most beautifully turned out, and of course her very slim figure is an advantage. Although I am quite thin, I feel almost a German frau beside Mona.

She had on the best-cut jhodpores I've ever seen, and a very smartly cut shirt and white linen sleeveless coat, like American girls wear.

She said to me:

"Hello, Maxine darling! Harry insisted on my taking some exercise. Are you surprised to see me?"

"Not very," I answered. "I know how obstinate you are when you want to do something."

She knew, of course, that I was referring to Harry, and she gave me an odd look. And I knew that she had made up her mind to marry him, and was determined to get him if she possibly could.

She and Harry mounted their horses, and we all rode along rather soberly, without saying anything.

Then, suddenly, I could not help seeing the funny side of it.

There were Mona and I, riding one each side of Harry, both of us very much in love with him, and for all we knew he might have been in love with the moon, and have no intention of taking any special notice of either of us.

I suddenly thought how absolutely ludicrous we were, and also I remembered the old adage of never running after a man, but letting him run after you.

So instead of being charming to Harry I thought I would be quite the opposite, for I saw that Mona was going to try and gush at him, and be her most seductive, sophisticated self.

"Well, I must not be tactless with you young things," I said, "I'm going to canter off."

I saw an annoyed expression on Harry's face, and he said:

"Don't be silly—don't go away, Maxine."

I said, in a complete imitation of Mona's manner:

"Darling, I hate being a gooseberry!"

With that I cantered away.

As I went, I heard Harry say again:

"Don't be so stupid, Maxine!"

Then Mona said something which I could not quite hear.

In spite of laughing as I left them, I felt absolutely savage, and furious, but I went on, and never looked back.

When I got right round the Park I stopped and dismounted and went back to the house, not waiting to see them again.

Now I am feeling miserable and I am sure Harry thought I was rude and disagreeable, and he'll like me less than ever, instead of more.

And I am sure Mona is saying beastly things about me, and that he will now know how unpleasant I can be.

I wish I had not been so stupid, but had stayed with them.

My only hope is that as I have gone away he'll wish I'd stayed, because I often feel like that about people.

If they are there, I don't notice them, but if they are not there I begin to think how amusing it would be if they were.

And here's a letter from Alec: what a surprise! But, oh dear, I really cannot attend to it . . . Harry and Mona . . . Mona and Harry . . . but it is all rather extraordinary!

Alec is going to get married to an American girl with absolutely piles of money. He's sailing for New York next week, and they are to be married over there.

So he's got his heiress after all, and I hope she enjoys him, with all his peculiarities, but I expect she wants an English husband with a title, and does not mind much about anything else.

This will give me something to talk to Harry about, and so I can make an excuse to see him again.

I do wonder what they said about me when I'd gone, and I wonder why Harry brought Mona this morning. I suppose because he wanted her.

I suppose also that he really is in love with her, so I might just as well forget all about him. The awful thing is that I don't think I shall ever forget him.

He seems to have always been in my thoughts, a sort of shadow behind everything these past three months, all the time, and I seem always to have been either madly in love with him or madly hating him.

But I never, never could be indifferent to Harry, like I feel about other people after an infatuation has ended.

I suppose it is an impossible dream, and after all the

182

quarrels we've had he could not possibly care for me again.

He has never said that he did, and yet I shall never forget the fact that he kissed me once.

When I am an old, old lady, and married to somebody else, I shall look back on that kiss as quite the most wonderful thing that ever happened to me.

People who say one always has to bear disappointments and crosses in one's life are quite right.

I suppose Harry is to be my cross in my life, and it does depress me terribly, because I feel I could never possibly kiss anyone else, or even think about them in that sort of way.

But I suppose I shall, sooner or later, only at the moment it seems impossible, because I want Harry so much.

REFLECTION FORTY-FIVE

Aunt Dorothy has sent for me.

"We are leaving for Scotland in a week, Maxine," she said. "I am going to take you to stay with your cousins, and then we will pay a few visits on the way south. There is just the chance that we may go to the Lido in the early part of September, which I know you will enjoy."

Of course I had to sound very pleased and excited, but really I am horrified!

We are leaving London a whole ten days sooner than I expected, and I don't want to go to the Lido at all—I want to go down to the South of France, but how can I suggest it without letting Aunt Dorothy guess why I want to go?

It wouldn't be very much fun to go with her if I want to see a lot of Harry. I don't know what to do about it all; oh, I am utterly miserable!

REFLECTION FORTY-SIX

I'm engaged . . . engaged! We're engaged!

I am not going to Scotland, because we're engaged!

It is all too wonderful and too exciting, and I am so desperately happy and I cannot believe it is true!

It is so thrilling that I want to remember every moment of what has happened and I am so afraid I shall forget how wonderfully it has all happened to me, and that I won't remember it.

If I have time, I shall have to write it all down, and keep it always by me, so that I shall never forget this biggest moment in all my life.

I was feeling so miserable and so desperate, after luncheon, and trying to make up my mind what I would do, when the telephone rang, and Harry said:

"Are you alone, Maxine? Can I come and talk to you?"

My heart simply jumped about with excitement, and I said:

"Of course . . . do come now."

I went upstairs to my room and changed my dress three times before I thought I looked really nice.

Luckily everyone had gone, and there was no one in the house except Aunt Dorothy, who was quite safe in her bedroom.

So I went downstairs, and waited in the little morning room.

Harry arrived and I think we were both a little embarrassed at first. He walked about, lit a cigarette, and then said suddenly:

"Were you angry about this morning, Maxine?"

"Of course not, Harry," I answered, "why should I be?"

But I don't think I said it very confidently, and he said:

"Mona insisted on coming—but that has nothing to do with it—I wish to God you did mind!"

I felt suddenly rather breathless, and I said, "Why?" in a silly, rather quavering voice.

He threw his cigarette away and sat down suddenly beside me on the sofa, and said:

"Because I love you, Maxine. The whole thing has been such a hopeless muddle since we first met, and there is so much for us both to explain to each other, that it's almost impossible to know where to begin.

"Perhaps I am wrong, and you do not care a damn about me, but from the very first moment I saw you, Maxine, I fell in love with you.

"I tried not to because you were so young and I thought I had no use for *débutantes*, but I could not help myself.

"I want to tell you now that since we met, I've never looked at another woman. It's true, although you mayn't think so—because circumstances were against me."

He got up, walked across the room, and went on talking:

"The night you saw me, things were not as you thought, Maxine—I'm not going to say any more, because it's not a subject either of us want to talk about—but I just wanted you to know."

I did not say anything, but just sat staring, and my heart was thumping, but I still could not believe what he was saying was true.

And then he came back to me and said:

"I love you, Maxine, and I want you to marry me. Please marry me, darling, and let's go away from all this, and forget all the times we have fought with each other!

"You attract me so terribly, with your wonderful hair, and your outlooks on life.

"You're so courageous, Maxine—it was so brave the

186

way you faced this extraordinary *ménage*. But, darling, I can't let you play about with these sort of people any longer.

"I want you to belong to me, and I want to be able to look after you."

And he said sort of pleadingly:

"You do love me a little, don't you, Maxine?"

And somehow there was no need for me to answer, because he kissed me.

It was like being swept up to the stars!

The world seemed to stand still, and nothing else mattered, or could ever matter again, except Harry.

"I love you," he said in a sort of hoarse voice. "God, how I love you!"

And he kissed me until I couldn't breathe, or think. I only knew that this was Heaven and much more wonderful than I ever thought it could be.

Then we talked and talked, and they came to say tea was ready, but we went on talking and forgot to go and have any.

Then at last I realised it was nearly seven o'clock, and I said:

"Oh, Harry . . . what will Aunt Dorothy say?"

"What can she say?" he asked.

I realised that she could not very well object without giving herself away, and I felt that Uncle Lionel would be quite pleased, once he knew how much in love Harry and I are with each other.

The wonderful thing is that Harry does not care a bit for Mona. He thinks she is quite nice, but he would not think of marrying her, and it's always been me that he wanted to marry from the very first moment.

Though he liked Aunt Dorothy very much, they both knew it was a kind of game, and he has not been a bit disloyal to her in ending it, because they always arranged that they would part without any recriminations on either side.

It was only a question of *passer le temps* for both of them.

That makes me feel very much better, because I am so wonderfully and divinely happy myself that I do not want anyone else to feel unhappy through me.

187

Not even Mona—but I am sure she will get over it quite quickly and find somebody else, because she is so pretty.

But Harry does not want to talk about her, only about me, and he kept on kissing me. Each time it was more thrilling than the last until he said:

"I adore every wonderful scrap of you and one day I'll kiss you from the top of your glorious red head to the soles of your tiny feet."

I was trembling because it's so exciting and all I could say was:

"Please, Harry, darling ... let's get married very ... soon."

Now Harry has gone to dress and is coming back to dinner here, and then he is going to tell Uncle Lionel. I shall leave it to Uncle Lionel to break the news to Aunt Dorothy.

That's very cowardly, but I really do not feel I can face her.

I am so frightfully excited and thrilled that I keep on forgetting to get undressed ready for my bath, but stand about looking at myself in the glass.

I do want to get more and more beautiful for Harry, and I want to get married quickly ... quickly, so that I can always be with him.

It is all so marvellous, I can't believe it's true!

I think I will pinch myself, like people do in books, to see if I'm really here!

I love him!

Even to say that makes me feel breathless and my heart thumps like it does when he kisses me.

I love him!

REFLECTION FORTY-SEVEN

It's all right—everything is settled. I've cabled Mummy.

Uncle Lionel has agreed, and so has Aunt Dorothy.

She kissed me, and said she hoped I'd be very happy, rather in the tone of voice that she'd be surprised if I was.

Still, she has been quite pleasant about it, and Uncle Lionel was delighted that I was so happy. I think he quite likes Harry.

After we had told them, Harry and I went out and danced.

I am afraid quite a lot of people at the Embassy must have guessed what had happened, because we both looked so radiant.

One or two people stared, and smiled as if they knew we were really in love with each other.

I did not mind a bit, because I want people to know how lucky I am, and that Harry is to belong to me—he says already I belong to him.

The wonderful thing is that he wants to live just as I planned I should like to, and we are to be in Warwickshire, or at his house in Scotland most of the time, and only come up to London occasionally, or in the Season.

He's very keen that first we should travel, and he says that before we settle down we must see a lot of the world.

We may not have an opportunity another time, or be quite free, unhampered by responsibilities.

Of course I knew by that he meant we might have children, whom we should hate to leave behind. It is too absurd, but I really felt like blushing.

Though I want to talk to Harry about everything, and tell him anything I think of saying, there is something awfully intimate about children, however much you love somebody.

Then because I really wanted to know, I asked:

"How does one ... have a baby ... nobody has ever told me?"

He looked at me strangely as if he couldn't believe I was telling him the truth.

Then he answered in a funny sort of voice.

"You really don't know! Oh, my perfect darling, you are so sweet, innocent and unspoilt. There is no one like you!"

He pulled me into his arms and held me very tightly, but he did not kiss me.

After a moment I said:

"You haven't answered my question ... is it ... something to do with ... kissing?"

He was silent for a moment as if he was thinking.

Then he said:

"Yes, my precious, it's the end of a long, long kiss, but I'll explain it to you when we've married."

"I would like you to do ... that," I told him.

Then he kissed me very slowly and very possessively, so that I felt as if I melted into him, and it was very wonderful!

We did not say anything more at the time, but as soon as we've been right round the world I shall insist on having a baby, because I know Harry is longing for an heir.

He has awfully serious ideas, which I never realised before, just like Uncle Lionel, about the responsibilities of money.

Between us, we shall be very rich, and he has all sorts of plans for things we can do to help people who are not as lucky as we are.

I feel that my life is just beginning, and that there is not only going to be a life of trying to be happy together, but also a life of trying to help to do some good in the world.

I am sure, if there is such a thing as an afterlife, and Ivor is there, he must approve of our ideas.

It's a funny thing, but when you are happy and in love, one seems to believe in all the things one thought of as a child.

Because I am so happy at the moment, I want to believe in God and Heaven and angels, and all the lovely things.

I think perhaps there is something in religion after all, because when you are very happy, or very unhappy, you always turn to it.

It is only when one is at the mediocre and indifferent stage of existence that one criticises and has the time to dissect one's emotions.

I keep on thanking God for giving me Harry, and I want to ask Him that we may always be as happy as we are now.

We couldn't be happier—it would be impossible.

I am to be married in the autumn. I shall have eight bridesmaids and four pages—of course at St. Margaret's, Westminster, and a lovely reception here afterwards.

And then we shall go somewhere quite quiet and alone for three or four days before we start on our honeymoon round the world.

I can imagine nothing more wonderful than seeing the world with Harry beside me and of course being alone ... with him.

He has read lots and lots and knows so much about everything, and he does not mind my being stupid and asking questions, and not knowing half the things I ought to.

In fact, I have a feeling he rather likes it, so it just shows that clever women aren't always a success with men.

I am going to have the most wonderful trousseau that anyone has ever had, so that I shall look perfectly lovely for him.

I want everything in my life to be perfect and beautiful, though I feel it's perhaps a little superficial to think of those things.

Yet I am sure they are important because after all

191

Poppy's first love affair only failed because everything around them was artistically wrong.

I cabled Poppy and Tommy because I know how excited they'll be, and I am going to ring them up to-morrow night, and tell them more.

The engagement is going to be announced in three or four days' time, just as soon as Aunt Dorothy and Harry can have time to write to all the relations and tell them what is happening because relations like to know before anyone else, or they are offended.

I am so wonderfully, wonderfully happy, and I feel I shall never sleep, because little shivers of excitement keep running all over me, right from my toes to my head.

I can still feel Harry's kisses, and that is enough to keep anyone awake, because they are the most thrilling things in the world.

I love him . . . I love him . . . I love him!

I want him to hold me in his arms and kiss me a thousand times.

I shall never be good enough for him but I will try . . . really hard . . . to be exactly as he wants me to be.

I am so lucky, so fantastically, marvellously lucky.

Oh, Harry, I do love you so much!

I am pretending he is here and I am close to him . . . and it won't be very long before it's true . . .

It makes me quiver to think of it, and a little flame seems to flicker inside me. It's so intense . . . it is half a wild sort of fantastic pleasure and half a pain.

Love is so much bigger than I expected and so much, much more marvellous.

I love Harry . . . I adore him . . .

Oh please, God, make him go on loving me for ever and ever!